C000173681

DEATH AT THE ANCHORAGE

A KIPPER COTTAGE MYSTERY

JAN DURHAM

INKUBATOR
BOOKS

Published by Inkubator Books
www.inkubatorbooks.com

Copyright © 2022 by Jan Durham

ISBN (eBook): 978-1-83756-036-3
ISBN (Paperback): 978-1-83756-037-0
ISBN (Hardback): 978-1-83756-038-7

Jan Durham has asserted her right to be identified as the author of this work.

DEATH AT THE ANCHORAGE is a work of fiction. People, places, events, and situations are the product of the author's imagination. Any resemblance to actual persons, living or dead is entirely coincidental.

No part of this book may be reproduced, stored in any retrieval system, or transmitted by any means without the prior written permission of the publisher.

1

'IS THERE ANYBODY THERE?' bellowed Iris Gladwell.
'REVEAL YOURSELVES!'

'Perhaps,' suggested Patricia Haddington, 'you should try not to shout. If there *are* any ghosts here, you'll be scaring them away.'

'WHAT ARE YOU TALKING ABOUT?' Iris glared at her. 'I'M NOT SHOUTING.'

Liz McLuckie gazed at the two old ladies and wondered what on earth she was doing there. She didn't believe in life after death, and certainly didn't believe that Ouija boards had mystical powers, and yet here she was, sitting in the Anchorage Retirement Home, curtains drawn in the middle of the afternoon, taking part in a séance.

It had all started that morning, when her friend Iris had received a call from the home, telling her a room had become available. Because Iris's son Irwin was away at a conference, Iris had asked Liz to drive her there. After taking a look at the room, they'd had tea with another of Iris's friends, Clara, who was already a resident. Clara told them she'd found a Ouija board in the games cupboard, and Iris suggested an

impromptu séance. Liz had been surprised – Iris was generally a no-nonsense kind of person – but she'd gone along
with it because she thought it couldn't hurt for Iris to meet
some of the other residents.

Now here they were – seven people gathered around a
Ouija board laid out on the long mahogany dining table. As
well as Liz, Iris and Clara, there was Patricia Haddington, a
tweedy woman in her seventies wearing a green padded gilet,
and three elderly gents – Dickie Ledgard, Roger Darnton and
Max Plum. Liz was surprised they'd all agreed to join in, but
she supposed there wasn't much else to do at the Anchorage
at that time of the day. They'd drawn the curtains to create a
suitably spooky atmosphere, although it was slightly undermined by the garish orange decor and the collection of
walking aids in the corner.

'I beg your pardon,' said Patricia, 'but you *are* shouting.'

'I AM NOT.'

Liz stifled a sigh. There was no point asking Iris to turn
down the volume – she was incapable of speaking at
anything less than a bellow.

'I don't think she's shouting,' said Dickie Ledgard. 'Is she
shouting?'

'She is,' said Max Plum. 'You can't tell because you're
deaf.'

'Only in one ear.'

'Perhaps,' Liz suggested diplomatically, 'Clara would like
to ask the questions?'

Clara darted her a grateful look, and then smiled at Iris.
'I'm happy to do it, if that's okay?'

Iris shrugged. 'WHATEVER.'

'Let's get on with it, shall we?' snapped Max, who was
wearing a bow tie and had a plummy accent to match his
surname. '*Antiques Roadshow* is on in half an hour and I don't
want to miss it.'

Everyone settled down, and put their fingers back on the planchette.

'Is there anybody there?' said Clara.

Silence, except the laboured breathing of Roger Darnton. From his grey complexion, Liz suspected he'd once been a heavy smoker.

Clara tried again. 'Is there anybody there? If so, please try to communicate with us.'

A noise came from under the table: a soft expulsion of air.

'Sorry.' Dickie Ledgard blushed. He was a wiry man who looked as if he could do with a good feed. 'It was the cucumber at lunchtime. Doesn't agree with me.'

'Doesn't agree with us either,' snapped Patricia. 'Please try to control yourself.'

'For heaven's sake! Are we going to do this or not?' Clara's assertiveness surprised Liz. She was very dainty, and looked as if she wouldn't say boo to a goose, but she obviously had a certain amount of authority in the group, because everyone fell silent.

'Is there anybody there?' repeated Clara. 'We're waiting to hear from you.'

There was an expectant pause, and then Liz felt the planchette shiver under her fingertips. It started to slide towards her, towards the alphabet on the table.

'It's moving!' hissed Clara.

'Someone's pushing it,' muttered Patricia.

'Not me,' said Max.

'Nor me,' said Dickie. He looked alarmed.

'I don't know why you're all so surprised,' muttered Roger Darnton. 'Isn't this what we're here for?'

'Shhh,' said Clara. She spelled out the letters as the planchette nudged at them. 'M... U... R... D...'

'I think that was the C,' interrupted Dickie.

'No, it wasn't,' said Clara. 'It was definitely the D.' The planchette was still moving. Clara continued. 'E... R...'

'Murder?' said Liz, her interest piqued.

'Shh,' hissed Clara. 'It's still going. E... R...'

'MURDERER!' bellowed Iris.

'Oh, for heaven's sake, this is ridiculous!' snapped Patricia. She took her fingers off the planchette. 'What are we, teenagers?'

Liz almost laughed out loud. At fifty, she was by far the youngest there. She guessed that Patricia's reluctance to continue was prompted by fear.

'Oh, come on,' said Clara. 'We've just got started. There's someone trying to tell us something. Let's try again.'

'OR ARE YOU A SCAREDY CAT?' suggested Iris.

Patricia glared her, but put her hand back on the board. Everyone else followed suit, some with more enthusiasm than others. Dickie seemed particularly apprehensive. Max, on the other hand, was pretty gung-ho about the whole thing, while Roger just looked bored.

The planchette moved again. Clara spelled out the message.

'M... U... R... D... E... R... E... R.'

Dickie frowned. 'Do they mean *they're* a murderer, or...'

'THAT SOMEONE HERE IS?' suggested Iris, gleefully.

The planchette was still moving, picking up speed.

"M... U... R... D... E... R... E... R... M... U... R...' Clara stopped reading the message aloud. She didn't need to. The planchette was whizzing from one letter to the next, spelling out the same word again and again.

'Who are you?' Clara called out.

It stopped suddenly. Then moved towards the letter E.

'Enough!' snapped Patricia. 'That's enough.'

'I agree,' said Roger. He stood up, breaking contact with the board.

Max raised his bushy eyebrows. 'Don't you believe in ghosts and ghoulies?'

'Oh, I believe in them, alright,' replied Roger, 'but Ouija boards are dangerous. If you're not careful, you can let any old entity in.'

'Entity?' repeated Dickie nervously.

'Malevolent spirit,' said Roger. From the smile that was playing around his lips, Liz suspected he was enjoying himself.

'Well, that's just dandy, isn't it?' blustered Max. 'You might have told us that before we started, don't you think?'

Roger shrugged.

Patricia strode to the window to open the curtains. They all blinked in the late afternoon light. 'I don't know about anyone else, but I have better things to do.' She stomped out.

'I think it's probably time we made tracks too, Iris,' suggested Liz. 'Nelson will be fretting.' It was true that Liz didn't like to leave her English bull terrier home alone for too long, but it was also true that she sometimes used him as an excuse to make a fast escape. At that particular moment, a fast escape was very appealing. Liz left Iris to say her good-byes to Clara, and went to wait in the car. Iris joined her before too long, grumbling to herself as she fastened her seat belt.

'Are you okay?' asked Liz.

'I'M FINE.'

'What do you think?'

'ABOUT WHAT?'

'The room.'

'IT'S TOO PINK.'

It was hard to argue with that; the room had been painted a vivid shade of salmon.

'BESSIE BARKER HAD NO TASTE.'

'Bessie who?'

'BARKER. SHE USED TO HAVE THAT ROOM. SHE DIED TWO WEEKS AGO. ALWAYS WORE PINK, SILLY BEGGAR.'

'You could paint it. The manager said they let residents decorate to their own taste.'

Iris just sniffed. Liz didn't push it. She knew her friend would just dig her heels in. Iris's son Irwin had confided to Liz that he'd be much happier if his mum wasn't living in her ramshackle cottage alone. That had surprised Liz. She had no idea how old Iris was – she could be anywhere between seventy or and a hundred – but she still worked as a changeover cleaner for many of the rental properties in the town, and never walked anywhere if she could march there. She seemed very self-sufficient, if not downright indestructible. Liz found it strange to think of her living in the Anchorage Retirement Home.

Set high on the West Cliff of Whitby, the Anchorage was a large Edwardian building on the sweep of Royal Crescent. Its many windows overlooked the promenade and the expanse of the North Sea beyond it. Being February, the sea was slate grey, and the promenade almost deserted, except for a few hardy dog walkers. In summer it was very different, bustling with families heading down to the beach and day-trippers keen to see the sights. Liz reversed out of the car park and headed for the East Cliff and home.

Whitby was a town of two halves. Most of the elegant pastel buildings on the West Cliff had been built in the Regency and Victorian eras, when the fishing village had burgeoned into a popular tourist resort. They fronted the town centre, and the majority of the town's shops, which then gave way to the more modern sprawl of housing estates, schools and sports centres. The East Cliff, on the other side of the harbour, was much older, a jumble of old fishermen's cottages with red tiled roofs, all piled together in a haphazard maze of narrow alleyways and yards. Above them, on the cliff top, stood St Mary's church and the gaunt ruins of the abbey, the inspiration for Bram Stoker's *Dracula* and a place of pilgrimage for thousands of modern-day goths.

The harbour divided these two very different worlds. Still a busy fishing port, it was home to several working trawlers and the fish market, a long, low building on the edge of the quayside. Facing the market, on the other side of the narrow road, were amusement arcades, restaurants and many seafood, souvenir and candy kiosks.

Liz drove over the narrow swing bridge, which was the only way to get over the harbour, and parked in her usual spot in the private section of the car park at Tin Ghaut. They had to walk from there, down the narrow cobbled thorough-fare of Church Street, lined with small shops selling souvenirs, books, ice cream and hand-made jewellery. Even on a grey February day, Church Street was busy. When she and Iris reached the end of the street, they stopped beside the wrought-iron gate that led to Neptune Yard, which lay in the shadow of the 199 stone steps that led steeply up to the abbey.

'So,' said Liz to Iris, 'are you going to give the manager a ring, let her know?' She deliberately didn't look into the dark-ness beyond the gate, half expecting to see a pair of malevo-lent yellow eyes staring back at her. That mystery had been solved at Halloween, but she still couldn't suppress a shiver whenever she was passing Neptune Yard.

'I SUPPOSE.'

'Is it a yes or a no?'

'NO.'

'Really?'

'DEFINITELY.' Iris grimaced. 'THEY'RE ALL A BUNCH OF LOONIES IN THERE.'

Liz really couldn't argue with that.

She said goodbye to Iris and headed home down Henrietta Street. It only took her a minute to get there. Home, for the time being, was Gull Cottage, which stood next to the other cottage she owned – Kipper Cottage – beside the famous smokehouse. Liz had bought the two eighteenth-century cottages after she'd taken early retirement from her job in Edinburgh following the death of her husband, Mark. It was her intention to renovate both, to live in one and rent out the other as holiday accommodation. It had taken her almost five months to get Kipper ready, but then a malicious fire had undone most of her efforts. She'd had to work through the winter to repair the damage, and had only just been able to welcome guests again – a lovely couple, Helen and Andrew, and their beautiful French bull dog, Hugo.

Gull Cottage was still unrestored. She had to jiggle the key in the ancient lock before it yielded with a creak, to the inevitable accompanying *yip yip* of her dog Nelson. Liz patted him as she hung her coat beside the door.

'Did you miss me?'

Nelson grinned at her, tongue lolling, and ambled back to his basket. He had a massive, coffin-shaped head, disproportionately small body, and a patch over one eye that gave him a piratical air. Some unkind people in the town had dubbed him the ugliest dog in Yorkshire, but Liz thought he was beautiful.

The same couldn't be said of her kitchen. Liz looked around it and sighed. Most of the fittings had been ripped out to make way for new units. Apart from the brand-new Aga-style stove and the kitchen table there was only a tiny fridge, a Belfast sink, and a chest of drawers with a microwave and kettle on top.

She spotted a note on the table.

Gone to the Duke. Walked Nelson at 4. Tuna pasta in the fridge if you want it.

N X

Liz sent up a silent prayer of thanks to her young lodger. Niall was a star. She would eat the tuna pasta, pour herself a glass of wine, then have a quiet night in with Nelson and her laptop, choosing bathroom tiles.

LIZ WOKE next morning in her attic room to the sound of frantic banging. Still dazed by sleep, she struggled at first to tell where the noise was coming from. Eventually she realised someone was pounding at her front door.

Yip! Yip! Yip! barked Nelson, alerting her from the kitchen. Liz could also hear a fainter *Yap! Yap! Yap!* She realised it must be Hugo, the Frenchie next door in Kipper Cottage.

She hurried to find her dressing gown and stumbled down the narrow wooden staircase. Nelson was jumping up at the door, so Liz used one hand to grab his collar and the other to open it.

Iris stood on the step, her hair still in curlers, and her cardigan bristling with labels – she'd put it on inside out. Seeing who it was, Nelson stopped barking and Liz was able to let go of his collar.

'What is it?' Liz gasped. 'Are you okay?'

Iris shook her head.

'SHE'S BEEN MURDERED!'

2

'Take a deep breath, and tell us all about it.' Liz caught Niall's wide blue gaze over the top of Iris's head. He was only wearing a jumper over his boxer shorts, and his dark hair was sticking up in tufts.

'THEY RANG ME,' said Iris. 'SAID SHE WAS DEAD.'

'Who?' mouthed Niall at Liz. She shrugged. Iris was sitting at the table with a stunned expression, like a bird that had flown into a window.

'Tea?' suggested Liz. Niall hurried to fill the kettle, as Liz knelt on the floor beside Iris's chair.

'Who's dead, Iris?'

Iris frowned with annoyance. 'CLARA! THEY SAID SHE'D BEEN MURDERED. THE POLICE ARE THERE.'

'Murdered? How? When?'

'WHAT YOU ASKING ME FOR? I HAVE NO IDEA.'

Liz looked at the old lady thoughtfully, then went upstairs to find her phone. It rang quite a few times before it was picked up.

'Mmm?' The voice on the other end was sleepy.

'Kevin. What's going on?'

'What?'

'At the Anchorage?'

'What are you talking about?'

'Clara Bendelow.'

'Who's Clara Bendelow?'

'A friend of Iris. She lives... lived... at the Anchorage Retirement Home. Apparently, she's just been murdered.'

'Really?'

'Don't you know?'

'It's my day off. You've just woken me up. Is Iris okay?

'I'm not sure. The Anchorage called her, but she's not making a lot of sense.'

'Okay. Leave it with me. I'll find out what's going on.'

When she got back downstairs, Iris was slurping tea under the watchful eye of a shivering Niall. Liz felt a flash of guilt. The heating had been disconnected in readiness for the new boiler. February wasn't the best time of year to be doing that kind of work, but she had no choice if she wanted Gull to be liveable by the summer.

'You'd better go and put some clothes on, Niall, or you'll freeze.'

Niall nodded and disappeared up the stairs in a flash of gangly white legs. Liz took a blanket off one of the kitchen chairs and draped it around Iris's shoulders.

'DON'T FUSS,' snapped Iris. 'I'M FINE.'

Liz caught Nelson's eye. They both knew she wasn't. The bull terrier had retreated to his basket and was now gazing fretfully at Iris like a mother hen. Liz went over and patted him.

'It's okay, sweetie. She'll be okay.'

She made herself a mug of tea with the hot water left in the kettle. Niall clattered back down the stairs a couple of minutes later.

'Anyone want some breakfast? I'm starving.'

He was always starving. He ate enough to keep a small army on the march, yet never seemed to put on weight. He sniffed experimentally at the loaf he found in the breadbin. 'This bread isn't too bad. And we have eggs.'

Liz realised she had no idea what time it was. It was still dark outside. She looked at her phone. 06.15.

'Not for me, thanks. It's a bit early. Iris?' She realised the old lady wasn't listening. 'Iris?'

'WHAT?'

'Do you want something to eat?'

'AT A TIME LIKE THIS? ARE YOU DAFT?'

Niall grimaced at Liz, and then patted Iris's shoulder. 'I'll make you something anyway. If you don't fancy it, that's grand. You don't have to eat it.'

Liz's phone rang. She hurried to pick it up.

'Kevin. Hi.'

'It's true. I don't know the details yet, but Flint's cancelled my day off, so I soon will. Is Irwin there? Do you want me to call him?'

'He's in Toronto.'

'Shit. Do you need a hand? Shall I call Dad?'

Liz's heart skipped a beat at the mention of Benedict. 'No, it's okay. Niall's here, and Tilly and Mags are probably up and about. We'll manage.'

'Okay. I'll call you later, when I know more.'

NIALL LEFT JUST after seven in his battered old Fiat for his commute to the museum at York, so Liz took Iris and Nelson to the Full Moon Café. Liz's friend Tilly and her wife Mags owned the café – a bohemian mix of coffee shop, bookstore and repository of new age artifacts – less than five minutes' walk from Henrietta Street. It had bookshelves and comfy

leather chairs at one end, and café tables at the other, decorated in a hotchpotch of antiques and found treasures. Even
though the café wasn't open, Tilly and Mags greeted them at
the door.

'Come in, come in.' Tilly's eyes were warm. She tucked a
stray strand of bleach-blonde hair into her bandana and
ushered them inside. She was wearing a floaty hippie skirt
and a skull and crossbones T-shirt, maybe not the most
sensitive sartorial choice under the circumstances, but Iris
didn't seem to notice. She allowed them to make a fuss of her
as they settled her at one of the tables, while Nelson scooted
off to find the plastic pig Mags kept for him behind the
counter.

'I'll get you some tea, shall I?' suggested Mags. With her
dark hair and quiet demeanour, Mags was yin to Tilly's extro-
vert yang. They were the perfect couple.

'AND A SCONE IF YOU HAVE ONE,' said Iris. In spite of
her protestations at not being able to eat, she'd still managed
to polish off the eggs Niall had made her. The shock of Clara's
death clearly hadn't affected her appetite.

'Do you want jam on it?' asked Mags.

Iris shrugged.

Mags and Tilly's eyes flew to Liz's in alarm. Iris usually
had unfathomable but very strict rules about when she could
and couldn't eat jam.

'I'll just put it on the side, shall I?' suggested Mags. 'Then
you can add it yourself if you want to.'

Iris nodded distractedly. Mags disappeared through the
beaded curtain into the kitchen. Tilly beckoned Liz over
behind the counter.

'Is she okay?' she whispered.

Liz shook her head. 'I don't think she is. I don't know how
close she and Clara were, but this has really knocked her
sideways.'

'SHE CALLED ME. LAST NIGHT,' declared Iris, to no one in particular. Liz and Tilly went to join her.

'Clara?' suggested Tilly.

'WHO ELSE WOULD I BE TALKING ABOUT?' Iris glared at Tilly. 'SHE WAS UPSET.'

'Upset how?' asked Liz.

Iris shook her head. 'SHE SAID SOMETHING TERRIBLE HAD HAPPENED.'

'Did she say what?' asked Liz, as gently as she could.

'SHE SAID SHE COULDN'T TELL ME OVER THE PHONE. WE WERE GOING TO MEET HERE THIS MORN-ING, AT TEN O'CLOCK. Iris glanced at the clock. It was still only eight thirty. The café wasn't due to open until ten. Iris blinked back tears.

'I'll get your tea,' said Tilly, clearly not knowing how to handle seeing Iris upset. Iris was unusually unflappable, if not downright impervious. Tilly hurried back to the counter to busy herself with the teapot. 'Do you want some, Liz?'

'Yes, please.' Liz sat beside Iris. She had Irwin's mobile number, but wasn't sure if she should call him. She didn't know what time it would be in Toronto, and she wasn't sure there was a lot he could do, anyway. It would only make him fret if he wasn't able to get back straight away.

It all felt a bit surreal, if she was honest. It was only a few hours since they'd had their fractious Ouija session at the Anchorage. Liz wondered how Clara had died, and realised it had to have been pretty dramatic for it to be declared a crime scene so quickly.

Mags came through the curtain with a plate of scones and put them on the table.

'Dig in,' she said. 'I baked a batch last night, so there's plenty.'

They all did as she suggested. The sound of their eating was interrupted a minute or two later by tapping at the door.

Liz looked up to see Detective Sergeant Kevin Ossett peering in through the glass. She hurried to let him in.

'WELL? WHO KILLED HER?' Iris spotted him.

'It's too early to tell, Iris. But we're working on it.' Kevin was in his early thirties, but looked younger, with his freshly-scrubbed features and pink cheeks. Tilly poured him some tea, but he refused a scone with a shake of his head.

'DID SHE SUFFER?'

'No. I don't think so.' Kevin's gaze brushed Liz's before it slid away. 'It was very quick.' His expression was carefully neutral as he bent to pat Nelson. He straightened up again, took a sip of his tea and pulled a face. 'No sugar, Tills?'

'Sorry, I forgot. There's some behind the counter. In the red bowl.'

Kevin took his mug and went to find the sugar. Liz followed.

'That bad, eh?' she whispered.

Kevin pulled a face. 'It could have been worse, I suppose. But still...not nice.'

'It was good of you to come and see Iris.'

'Well, I was worried about her, but also...' He hesitated. 'I have an ulterior motive.'

'Oh?'

'We need someone to identify the body. Usually the Anchorage staff would do it, but under the circumstances...'

'They might be suspects?'

'I wouldn't put it exactly like that, but we'd rather not muddy the water.'

'Doesn't Clara have any family?'

'Just a niece.' He corrected himself. '*Grand*-niece. But she's off trekking somewhere. Nepal, we think. We haven't managed to track her down yet. We could identify Clara through dental records, but that would take a while. Do you think Iris...?'

'No. Absolutely not.' Liz lowered her voice even further. 'I don't think she's up to it.'

'Oh.' Kevin looked at Liz for a long moment. Hopeful.

She sighed. 'I suppose I could, if you're really desperate.'

KEVIN DROVE her to the police station, an unlovely brown brick building to the south of the town centre. Liz knew it well. Since coming to Whitby five years before, she'd spent much more time there than was respectable.

Unusually, the public waiting room was empty. Kevin pointed to one of the plastic chairs.

'Have a seat for a minute. I'll go and see if we're ready for you.'

Liz inspected the noticeboard while she waited. It was full of depressing public information posters about keeping your home secure, identity theft and victim support groups. She jumped as a woman barged in the door and marched up to the screened counter. The woman had dark bobbed hair, a sharp trouser suit and even sharper features. The overall effect of stylish super-efficiency was only slightly undermined by her neon Adidas trainers.

'There's a squad car in my space again,' she snapped to the female officer behind the counter. 'Get someone to move it.' The woman turned and spotted Liz. Her eyes widened.

'Good morning, DI Flint,' said Liz.

Flint scowled. 'What are you doing here?'

'I'm here to identify a body.'

'Not...?'

'Clara Bendelow.'

Kevin came back into the waiting room. Flint turned on him.

'Ossett. Is there really no one else who could identify our victim? Someone... anyone else?'

'People were hardly falling over themselves to do it. Mrs McLuckie's been very generous to offer... ma'am.'

The 'ma'am' was clearly an afterthought. Flint narrowed her eyes at him.

'I really don't mind,' said Liz. 'Public duty and all that.'

Flint muttered something under her breath that sounded very like an expletive and stomped back out the main door.

'Someone got out of bed on the wrong side this morning,' muttered Liz.

'Does her bed have a right side?' Kevin held the internal door for Liz to go through. 'This way.'

'I don't understand. Aren't we going to the morgue?'

Kevin grinned. 'We're not living in the dark ages. Or a TV drama. You don't actually have to look at the body.'

'Really?'

'Photographs.'

'Oh.' If she was honest, Liz would have liked to see Clara's body. Realistically, of course, she knew she wasn't likely to spot anything the police had missed, but...yes, she was a tiny, teeny bit disappointed. She could admit that ghoulish truth to herself, even if she would never admit it to anyone else.

Kevin showed her into an interview room.

'Morning, Mrs Mac.' Constable Bill Williams, known by his colleagues as Double Bill, rose to his feet as they entered. 'How are things?'

'I have had better starts to the day.'

'Ah... yes.' William's naturally mournful features grew even more mournful. 'Sorry. Stupid thing to ask, really.'

'Not at all. I'm actually quite well, all things considered.'

'Shall we get on with it?' suggested Kevin.

They all sat at the chipped Formica table, and Williams gave Kevin a folder.

'Sure you're okay with this?' Kevin asked Liz.

She nodded. 'Quite sure.'

He passed her several photographs of Clara, taken from various angles. Liz stared at them. Clara lay on a steel gurney with a sheet drawn up to her collarbone, eyes closed. If it wasn't for her unnatural pallor, and the fact Liz knew better, she'd have thought the old lady was sleeping.

'Can you formally identify the woman in the photographs as Clara Bernadette Bendelow?' asked Kevin.

'I can.' She hesitated. 'But... I thought you said she didn't go peacefully?'

'Mmm.' Kevin nodded. 'I wasn't really talking about the way she died – we think she was suffocated. I was talking about the fight she obviously put up while it was happening. The room was a mess.'

'I see.' Liz was very sorry to hear that. Kevin had been right not to mention it to Iris. 'Do you think it was a burglary?'

Kevin shook his head. 'She had jewellery and stuff lying around. Nothing worth very much, but a thief would definitely have taken it.'

'You would think,' mused Williams, 'that the killer might have at least staged it to look like a burglary? To throw us off the scent?'

That was a very good point. Liz looked at Williams thoughtfully. With his methodical way of speaking, and long, lugubrious features, he sometimes gave the impression of being a bit slow, but Liz knew he was actually much brighter than most of his colleagues.

'Perhaps it was an impulse killing?' she suggested. 'Spur of the moment? Which means it was probably someone at the Anchorage.'

'You're getting ahead of yourself there,' admonished Kevin. 'Way ahead.'

Liz realised he was right. Which was a pity.

Kevin was watching her closely. 'You know what I'm going to say now, don't you?'

'That I shouldn't get involved?'

'Exactly.'

Liz stared down at the photos of poor Clara, so shockingly white and silent. 'It's a bit late for that, don't you think?'

3

The next morning Liz was woken by the sound of the foghorn, blaring dolefully over the rooftops. She could usually see the tower of St Mary's church, high on the cliff above her, but today all she could see was a sheen of pearly grey. She did, however, hear the church bell strike six o'clock, its usually strident sound muffled and eerie. There was no point trying to go back to sleep – Nelson rarely slept past 6.30 and demanded a walk as soon as he woke up – so she just lay for a while, savouring the warmth of her bed. She didn't like mornings. There was always a gut-wrenching moment, just as she became aware of her surroundings, when she remembered that Mark was dead. He'd been dead more than five years now, but that waking realisation still caught her off guard, every morning. Lately, however, it seemed as if it had changed slightly. Not lessened exactly, but softened. Perhaps it was because of her friend, Benedict. Benedict, with his lean cyclist's body and his warm, intelligent gaze.

'Oh for heaven's sake.' Liz swung her legs out of bed, impatient with herself. There was no point thinking about

Benedict, who only saw her as a friend. There had been one moment, at Christmas, when she thought she'd seen a spark of something else in his eyes, but she had never seen it again, and so had dismissed it as her imagination. He'd been acting a little strangely ever since. Liz put it down to the fact that his ex-girlfriend, the Reverend Gillian Garraway, had left Whitby in the middle of January. Liz knew that Benedict still carried a torch for her.

Shivering, she pulled on underwear, jeans and a jumper, and carefully negotiated the rickety stairs down to the kitchen. Gull Cottage had two rooms on each floor, unlike Kipper Cottage next door, that only had one room per storey. Like Kipper, each floor in Gull was connected by a narrow wooden staircase enclosed in a cupboard. The cottages reminded Liz of little wooden ships, which wasn't really surprising, as Whitby had been built by seafaring people – fishermen, whalers and sailors.

Nelson greeted her with a wag of his stumpy tail and headed straight to scratch at the front door. Liz pulled on her overcoat and salt-stained boots.

'NIALL!' She yelled up the stairs. 'You'd better get up or you'll be late for work.'

She clipped Nelson on his lead and they went out.

It was still dark and the fog wrapped itself around them, so thick she could almost taste it. It smelled of the sea. They headed towards the abbey steps, and reached them in less than a minute.

Lit eerily by an old Victorian street lamp, the steps vanished up into the fog like the rope in an Indian rope trick. There were 199 in total, winding their way up to the ruin of the once great Benedictine Abbey on the clifftop. They were wide and shallow, worn smooth by innumerable feet through the centuries. She started to climb, leading Nelson carefully, knowing the steps would be particularly slippery that morning with moisture from the fog and the freezing temperature.

Liz always counted the steps on her way up, although it really wasn't necessary, as every tenth step was marked with a Roman numeral. Half way up she stopped to catch her breath on one of the wider coffin steps, so called because they allowed pall-bearers to take a rest on their way up to the church. Usually, on a dark winter morning, she'd be able to see the lights of the old town immediately below her, and the lights of the harbour itself. This morning, however, all she could see were the dozen steps she'd just climbed, and a ghostly half-light around the nearest street lamp. Everything else was obscured by the mist.

Nelson tugged on his lead, eager to get to the clifftop. Liz allowed him to pull her up the remaining steps, and then turned left at St Caedmon's Cross and headed into St Mary's churchyard. When Liz let Nelson off the lead he zipped off like an ungainly bullet, in search of rabbits, vanishing almost immediately from sight. Rather than trying to walk around the church as she normally did, and risk breaking her neck in the tussocky grass, Liz decided to wait for him where she was.

She took a deep breath as the atmosphere of the place started to seep into her. Ordinarily, she wasn't affected by Whitby's famously spooky vibes. Considered by many to be one of the most haunted towns in England, Whitby was the source of many chilling tales, as well as its most famous literary appearance in *Dracula*. But Liz didn't believe in ghosts. She couldn't deny, however, that she was feeling strangely unsettled. Was it the fog? Or was it Clara Bende-low's death? She tried to push away the image of the old lady's dead white face, but her thoughts kept returning to it, and to the séance they'd held at the Anchorage.

Someone had definitely been pushing the planchette. Was the word they spelled out – *murderer* – connected to

Clara's death? If it wasn't, it was a hell of a coincidence. Which meant... what? That someone at the séance had murdered Clara? Who? Liz could safely rule out Iris, which left Patricia Haddington, Dickie Ledgard, Max Plum and Roger Darnton. Were any of them really capable of such a thing?

Liz's thoughts were suddenly interrupted by a whimper, somewhere off in the fog. She strained to listen, but heard nothing more.

'Nelson?'

No response.

'NELSON!' His name was bounced back to her by the fog. But then, after a moment, a small shape detached itself from behind one of the gravestones and came trotting towards her. He was shaking his head from side to side.

'What's the matter?' She bent to examine him. His nose looked red and swollen. Had he accidentally run into one of the gravestones? Liz gently rubbed at it. 'You daftie. Come on, let's go home.'

For once, Nelson didn't resist. Rather than go back down the steps, Liz decided they should walk down the cobbled donkey path that descended at a lower level beside them. It was still steep, but a lot less slippery.

When they reached the bottom, a figure in a high-vis jacket emerged from Church Street. It was Mike Howson, the fishmonger, dragging his cart of fresh herrings to Fortune's smokehouse.

'Mornin', Mrs Mac!'

'Morning, Mike.'

'Wotcha, Nelson.' Mike took in Nelson's subdued air. 'What's up with your lad this morning?'

'I think he's just head-butted a gravestone.'

'Oh dear.' Mike chortled. 'I've just the thing for that.' He bent to scoop some of the ice that was packed around his herring, and gently held it against Nelson's nose for a moment or two.

'There now. Is that better?'

Nelson licked Mike's hand, and they all walked down Henrietta Street together.

'Brrr.' Mike shuddered 'This fog's a bugger, isn't it? Soaks right through. I'm frozen to the bone. Not good for an old man like me.'

Liz smiled. Mike was only a few years older than she was, in his early fifties. She knew he was fishing. She took the bait.

'Fancy a coffee and a warm up when you've dropped those off?'

'Don't mind if I do.' Mike grinned. 'Give me a minute and I'll be right with you.'

Liz let herself into Gull Cottage, unclipped Nelson, fed him and put the kettle on. She was wondering whether to give Niall another shout, when she heard a thump upstairs and realised she didn't need to. The water was almost boiled when Mike knocked on the door. She let him in and took his coat.

'They're having trouble lighting the fires next door this morning,' he said. 'Everything's that damp.'

Situated beside Kipper Cottage, the smokehouse was world famous for its delicious kippers, and was one of Mike's regular customers. Mike owned a popular wet fish shop on Baxtergate, on the other side of the harbour, where he lived with his wife and two strapping sons. He seemed to know everyone in the town, mainly because he was genuinely interested in people, but also because he *loved* to talk.

'I suppose you've heard about Clara Bendelow, up at the Anchorage?' said Liz, as she handed him his coffee. Now it was *her* turn to fish.

Mike nodded. 'Bad business. She was a lady, Mrs Bendelow. Always had a smile and a word.'

'Had she always lived in Whitby?'

'Born and bred, same as me. Her and her brother.'

'Her brother?' Liz was puzzled. Hadn't Kevin said Clara's only family was a grand-niece? 'He's dead, I take it?'

'Well, now...' Mike's eyes shone with a tale to be told. 'He's certainly *supposed* to be.'

Liz frowned. 'I don't understand.'

Mike settled himself more comfortably in his chair. 'Mrs Bendelow's brother, Eddie, was quite a character. Not a bad lad, but highly strung. A mischief-magnet, you know?'

Liz knew. She was something of one herself. She never went looking for trouble, yet somehow it always managed to find her.

Mike took a slurp of his coffee. 'To cut a long story short, sometime in the late 80s – '89, I think it was – Eddie went missing. No one was surprised at first. Everyone knew he owed money around the town, and just assumed he'd done a moonlight flit.'

'But he hadn't?'

Mike shook his head. 'A few weeks later, they found his clothes behind one of the beach huts on the West Cliff. Underpants and all. His credit cards and driving licence were there, too. A couple of weeks after that, they found one of his shoes, washed up at Sandsend. It was a long, drawn-out business, but the coroner eventually ruled it an accidental death. No note, you see. His mum was a widow. She passed away not long after. Everyone reckoned the distress of not knowing the fate of her only son simply broke her heart.'

'And they never found a body?'

'Never. But, there again, they weren't likely to. The currents around here are strong. If he'd swum out far enough, they'll have swept him all the way to Scandinavia.'

'How sad.'

Mike looked grim. 'I don't know what I'd do if one of my lads went like that. Doesn't bear thinking about, to be honest.'

They both jumped as Niall clomped down the stairs.

'Got to dash. I'm late.' He spotted their visitor. 'Morning, Mike.'

'Morning.'

'Have you had any breakfast?' Liz asked. She didn't think he had – there were no dirty dishes in the sink or crumbs on the table.

'No time!' Niall wrestled himself into his duffle coat and tugged his hat on. He looked around. 'I don't suppose the post's come yet?'

'It's still too early. Are you expecting something?'

'Special delivery. Can you sign for it when it gets here?'

'Course.' Liz was intrigued. 'What is it?'

Niall grinned. 'I'll show you tonight. Bye, Nelson. Bye, Mike.' Then he was off, out the door.

'I do like that lad,' said Mike. 'There again, I've never met an Irishman I didn't.'

'Me neither.' Liz had taken Niall under her wing the summer before, after he'd been fired from an archaeological dig up at the abbey. It turned out he'd been somewhat flexible with the truth when it came to the qualifications on his CV – hardly a hanging offence, in Liz's opinion – but the curator of the museum, Dora Spackle, had used it as an excuse to get rid of him. Liz had offered him somewhere to stay while he sorted himself out, and he'd helped her with the renovations at Kipper Cottage. Since then, he'd been a regular visitor, and now he had a job at the Castle Museum in York, he was staying on a semi-permanent basis. The town had taken Niall to its bosom, and the feeling seemed to be mutual.

Mike drained his mug and stood up. 'Thanks for the brew.'

'You're very welcome.'

When he'd gone, the cottage felt very quiet. Liz washed the mugs, and thought about Clara, so calm and ladylike. She'd never given any hint of the tragedy in her past. It just went to show that you never had any real idea what was going on in other people's lives.

4

L iz had a busy morning after that. Eric, the heating engineer, arrived just after nine to connect the new boiler. A few minutes later, the postie knocked at the door and Liz had to sign for Niall's delivery, an intriguing cylindrical package. Iris arrived at eleven for a cup of tea and cake. She didn't stay long.

'GOT TO GET ON,' she said, around her final mouthful of ginger sponge. 'I STILL HAVE THIMBLE AND ADVEN-TURE TO DO.'

Liz was surprised. 'Surely you're not doing changeovers today?'

'WHY WOULDN'T I BE?'

'You've had an awful shock. With Clara and everything.'

'DON'T BE DAFT.' Iris stood up. 'THE BAIRNS CAN'T FEED THEMSELVES, YOU KNOW.'

Liz smiled. Iris was speaking figuratively. She had no 'bairns' depending on her. Her only son, Irwin, was in his early forties. But Liz knew what she meant. Iris liked to earn her own money. The fact she was still working at her age (whatever that was) was proof of her fierce independence.

Liz saw Iris out, then made Eric a cup of tea.

'How are you getting on?' she asked the bottom half of his overalled body, which was sticking out of a hole in the floorboards. It took him a moment or two to extricate himself.

'I'll be up and running by end of play.' He brushed off his overalls and took the mug of tea. 'It'll be nice to get some heat in here, eh?'

'Awesome!' Niall hung up his duffle coat and skipped experimentally around the kitchen, watched by a bemused Nelson. 'I've never known it so warm in here!'

'I know,' said Liz, who was busy at the kitchen table. 'Great, isn't it?'

He peered at her. 'What in God's name are you doing with those peppers?'

'Stuffing them?'

'With what?' He frowned in disbelief. 'Cream cheese?'

'I thought it would be nice.' Liz had to admit that cooking wasn't her strong point. There was always something else she'd rather be doing.

'Don't we have mushrooms in the fridge, and that jasmine rice left over from yesterday?'

'I think so.'

'Okay.' He shooed her away from the peppers. 'Leave it to me.' He looked around. 'But first...'

He spotted his cylindrical package beside the door, pushed the pepper prep board carefully to one side and lifted the package onto the table.

'Can you guess what it is?' he asked.

'A giant can of baked beans?'

He gave her a gleeful look, and then tore off the brown paper wrapping. There was a box inside, with a label on the side that read – Armstrong's Vintage Clothing. He took off the lid, and pulled out what was inside...a top hat. He examined it in the light.

'Late 1800s, they reckon. It's a beauty, isn't it?'

Liz had to agree. It was as black as a beetle, and as glossy as a thoroughbred horse. Magisterial. But...

'Why?' she asked.

'For my new job.'

'At the museum?'

'My new *part-time* job.'

'You're giving up the Duke?'

'Of course not.' He put the hat on his head, struck a dramatic pose and adopted a deep, cultured English accent. 'Meet Doctor Darke, your guide to Whitby's bloody past and spooky present. Come with me into the labyrinthine heart of the town and I shall introduce you to witches, demon dogs and ghostly monks.' He reverted to his own voice. 'Cameron Tufnall's asked if I can help him with his tours. He has more bookings than he can manage, and doesn't want to turn people away.'

It didn't surprise Liz that Cameron had asked Niall to help. Niall was a natural storyteller, always ready with a stream of tales about his extended family. He was also a convincing showman, as she knew all too well from the events of the previous Halloween. But it worried her that he was spreading himself too thin.

'How are you going to manage three jobs?' She didn't want to remind him that he'd also promised to help her with renovations in lieu of rent.

'I'll be fine. I have to get Frannie through her MOT.'

Frannie was Niall's elderly Fiat. Ensuring she was always fit to drive was an expensive business.

'I worry about you,' said Liz, as Niall went to the fridge, still wearing his top hat. 'You know what they say about all work and no play.'

'I do. And it's true.' Niall looked glum and tapped himself on the chest. 'This Jack's a very dull boy. My love life's abysmal. Dead in the water, in fact.'

Liz hadn't really been talking about his love life, but was quite flattered he felt comfortable enough to discuss it with her. She watched as he washed his hands in the sink.

'I don't know how I'm ever going to meet someone.'

'You could go online? Dating apps?'

'Not my cup of tea. I'm not after a fling. I want to meet someone I *really* like. Someone who *really* likes me. Fat chance of that, the way things are just now. Sure, I might as well be one of those ghostly monks up at the abbey.'

Liz knew exactly how he felt.

'SHE WAS DEFINITELY SUFFOCATED,' said Kevin. 'The autopsy results confirmed cause of death this morning. Asphyxiation.'

'Poor Clara,' said Liz. There was never a good way to be murdered, of course, but that seemed a particularly distressing way to go.

She was playing Mah-jong with Kevin, Benedict and Tilly in Benedict's conservatory. Benedict lived in what locals called the 'posh' part of town, by Pannet Park. He had a big Edwardian house, set back from the road and screened by a beech hedge, with glorious views of the park. The conservatory that led from the kitchen was a proper Victorian glass house, with tropical plants and wicker furniture. It was also the favourite snoozing spot for many elderly cats, a legacy from Benedict's late wife Katherine.

'Does Iris know yet?' asked Tilly.

'Not as far as I know,' said Kevin. 'I've been keeping out of her way, to be honest. I really don't want to be the one to tell her.'

'She'll hear about it soon enough anyway,' said Benedict.

His grey-streaked hair was the only thing that betrayed his fifty-something years, otherwise he was lean and athletic, almost boyish-looking. 'It's just a matter of time.' Everyone knew he was right. News travelled fast in Whitby, and bad news faster than any.

'Surely it would be better if one of us told her?' said Tilly.

For some reason, everyone looked at Liz.

'Why does it always have to be me?' She sighed. 'Okay. I'll have a word with her in the morning.' She looked at the tiles in her hand. 'Whose turn is it?'

No one could remember.

Typically, their games were fiercely contested, but tonight nobody was in the mood. Liz would never have admitted it, but Thursday's Mah-jong nights were the highlight of her week, because she overcame her usual aversion to catering and helped Benedict make supper before the others arrived. Earlier that afternoon, however, Benedict had phoned her to suggest he buy a Chinese takeaway today instead. He'd had a tiring day getting a new exhibit ready for the museum – he managed the Captain Cook Maritime Museum on Grape Lane. Liz, always slightly paranoid where Benedict was concerned, had wondered whether it wasn't just an excuse not to be alone with her.

'Did anything else come up in the autopsy?' asked Tilly.

Kevin shook his head. He tried to feign nonchalance, but only succeeded in looking enigmatic.

Tilly clapped her hands. 'Something *did*, didn't it?'

'You do know this is police business?' he snapped. 'I don't want to go spreading it about to all and sundry.'

'All and sundry?' Tilly looked affronted.

'Alright... to be specific, I don't want to go spreading it to Liz.'

Everyone looked at her.

'Are you saying you don't trust me?' she asked, shocked.

'Of course not. I'm saying *Flint* doesn't trust you. She'd burst a blood vessel if she thought I was telling you anything at all about this investigation.'

'She's just jealous,' said Tilly, 'because Liz is a better detective than she is.'

'I wouldn't go that far,' said Liz. 'I just like to help when I can.' She looked at Kevin with a wounded expression.

He threw up his hands in surrender. 'Okay! I give up.'

'So?' prompted Tilly.

'The examination found tissue – epithelials – under Clara's fingernails. We think she scratched her attacker when she was fighting them off.'

'Good for her,' said Tilly.

Liz was thoughtful. If the killer was going around with scratches that would surely make him – or her – easier to spot. She realised she hadn't seen any of the séance participants since Clara's death.

'Oh!' exclaimed Tilly.

'What is it?' asked Liz, alarmed.

'I've been sitting on a pong of dragons all this time and never noticed.'

Benedict sighed. 'I don't think any of us are concentrating, are we? Let's just bring this game to a close and call it a night.'

After they'd finished and acknowledged Kevin as the winner, they helped Benedict clear the table and the kitchen. Kevin buttonholed Liz as she was scraping the leftovers of their Chinese meal into the composting bin.

'Can I ask your advice about something?'

'Course.'

'It's Valentine's Day next week.'

It hadn't been on her radar at all, but Liz realised he was right.

'It's my first one with Anna, and I have no idea what to get her... Jewellery, maybe?'

Liz pulled a face. Mark had often bought her something small and sparkly for the fourteenth of February. In fact, the earrings she was wearing – tiny ruby studs – had been a Valentine's gift from him. But they'd known each other very well.

'If I were you, I'd play safer for your first year,' she said. 'Jewellery's very subjective.'

'So, what then? Chocolates? Flowers? Aren't they a bit lame?'

'Chocolates, definitely. But flowers...it very much depends on what they are. Nobody would thank you for a bunch of carnations, but you can order some really gorgeous flowers online.'

'I dunno. It still seems a bit of a cop-out.'

'Think of something small to go with them. Small, and meaningful...Does she like animals?'

Kevin thought for a while. 'She likes ducks.'

'Ducks?'

He nodded. 'She has a few duck ornaments. And a rubber duck in the bathroom.'

Liz had an idea. 'You could buy her a Lucky Duck!'

Lucky Ducks were very much a Whitby thing, made for generations in a little glass workshop on Sandgate. Liz had spent many a happy hour watching the craftsmen making them when she was on her school holidays. She'd even had a little collection of her own that she'd bought with her pocket money.

'You could get her a red one,' she suggested. 'For Valentine's.'

'Have you finished with the compost bin?' Benedict joined them, and immediately picked up that he'd interrupted something. 'You two look very conspiratorial. Should I be worried?'

'Liz has just had a great idea what I should get Anna for Valentine's Day.'

'Oh.' Benedict frowned. His eyes met Liz's and she saw something there. A flicker of some emotion. He looked away again and pointed to the bin. 'If you're done with that, I'll put it out.'

She tried not to look disappointed as she closed the lid and passed it to him. 'There you go.'

She watched him as he took it outside. She'd definitely seen something in his eyes. Something she'd never seen before. But what, exactly?

5

Iris's cottage – Benbow Cottage – was in Neptune Yard, one of more than eighty 'yards' still left in Whitby. To step into one was to catch a glimpse of what the fishing town must have been like in its heyday, with dozens of families living huggermugger together, sharing the same washhouse, toilet and drying area. Neptune Yard was accessed by a narrow alleyway at the bottom of the abbey steps, guarded by a wrought-iron gate. Inside, there were half a dozen cottages, arranged in a higgledy-piggledy fashion, some side-on and some facing each other across the square. At the furthest end there was a small, fenced allotment. It was all very neat and well cared for, but Liz knew it had once been overcrowded and insanitary, a hotbed of disease and dirt. So much for the 'good old days.'

She knocked on the door of Benbow Cottage, which was the first in the yard. The anchor knocker had been recently polished, but the paint on the door was peeling, and the bullseye pane was cracked. There was no answer, so Liz knocked again.

'HANG ON A MINUTE.' Iris's voice came from inside.

'KEEP YOUR RUDDY HAIR ON.' Eventually, the door opened. 'CAN'T A WOMAN HAVE A PEE IN PEACE?'

'Sorry, I didn't think you were in.'

Iris ushered Liz inside, and looked pointedly at the white box Liz was carrying.

'I've brought cake,' said Liz.

Iris brightened. 'I'LL PUT THE KETTLE ON.'

Liz sat on one of the rickety kitchen chairs while Iris busied herself with the kettle. The kitchen could have fallen straight from the pages of a Dickens novel, with a huge black range, and open shelving lined with jars of home-made preserves. The gas stove was decades old, almost as ancient as the ones she'd taken out of her own cottages. It took Iris several attempts to get a burner to light.

'Are you sure that's safe?' asked Liz.

'SAFE AS HOUSES. THE IGNITION WHATSIT JUST NEEDS A NEW THINGAMABOB.' Iris plopped teabags into a teapot. Liz took a deep breath.

'Clara's post mortem came in yesterday,' she said.

Iris stopped what she was doing to fix her with a gimlet eye. 'AND?'

'And she was suffocated.'

'WHAT WITH?'

'I don't know. Kevin didn't say.'

Iris turned back to the teapot. Liz wondered whether she should tell her about the fight Clara had put up, and decided not to. She didn't want to distress her any further.

'I'M BETTING SHE DIDN'T GO QUIETLY,' said Iris.

Liz winced. In spite of her eccentricities, the old lady was as sharp as a tack. But Liz didn't know what to say to that. Luckily, the phone rang.

'WHO ON EARTH CAN THAT BE?' Iris stomped into the living room to answer it. 'YES, THIS IS IRIS GLADWELL, WHO ARE *YOU*?... OH, HELLO, MRS BAXTER.'

Liz immediately wondered why Violet Baxter, the manager at the Anchorage, was calling. She didn't need to eavesdrop – she could have heard Iris's end of the conversation if she'd been standing on the abbey steps.

There was a long pause while Iris listened to what Mrs Baxter had to say.

'IT DEPENDS ON WHETHER SOMEONE CAN BRING ME. I'LL SEE WHAT I CAN DO.'

Iris came back into the kitchen with a troubled expression. 'THAT WAS MRS BAXTER UP AT THE HOME. SHE'S ASKED ME TO GO AND GET CLARA'S THINGS.'

LIZ PULLED into the car park at the Anchorage with a feeling of foreboding. Iris had been unusually quiet on the way there, and was sitting white-faced and silent in the passenger seat.

'You could have let me do it, you know,' said Liz. 'I really don't mind.'

'SHE WOULDN'T WANT A STRANGER GOING THROUGH HER THINGS.'

Liz didn't take offence. Privately, she thought Mrs Baxter and her team were a little too eager to get rid of every trace of their unlucky resident. It seemed disrespectful. But perhaps it would be better for the other residents not to have to see Clara's things.

'Just out of interest,' asked Liz, in an attempt at conversation, 'how long have you known Clara?'

Iris shrugged. 'NOT THAT LONG.'

'Really?'

Iris just harrumphed and gave Liz nothing more. Liz was glad to get out of the car and go inside.

Violet Baxter greeted them in reception.

'Thank you so much for doing this.' She was a tall woman

with tightly curled black hair and a harried expression. Liz supposed the last few days couldn't have been easy for her. 'We really do appreciate it.'

'LET'S JUST GET ON WITH IT,' grumbled Iris. She headed for the stairs.

Liz lingered beside Mrs Baxter. 'I have to say, I'm not really sure she's up to it. Couldn't you have put Clara's things in storage somewhere until her niece gets here?'

'We don't really have the space. And we have two people coming this afternoon to look at the room.'

Personally, Liz wouldn't be so keen to jump into a dead person's shoes, but she supposed that was par for the course in a retirement home. Still, it was unlikely that the Anchorage would tell anyone how Clara had died. So far it hadn't been in the newspapers. Ever since the *Whitby Bugle* had lost their star reporter in the autumn, they'd been a little slow to pick up local news. In this case, it was probably for the best, at least as far as the Anchorage was concerned.

'We'll be having tea and coffee in the sitting room at eleven, if you'd like to join us after.'

Clara's room, so warm and welcoming just a few days before, had been stripped. The lace and velvet curtains had gone, and so had Clara's beautiful embroidered bed linen. The walls and mattress were bare. There were no remaining signs of Clara's personality, or the fact that the room had recently been a crime scene, apart from a single evidence marker on the window sill. All Clara's belongings had been stacked in a corner. There wasn't much: a couple of bin bags of clothes, a few pictures, two small boxes of ornaments, a pile of bed linen and a shoebox.

It only took Liz and Iris fifteen minutes to get them into the car.

'Mrs Baxter says there's tea if we want it, but we don't have to stay if you'd rather get away.'

Iris brightened. 'I'M GAGGING FOR A BREW.'

The communal sitting room was a large, bright room with a fireplace at one end and French doors into the garden at the other. It had comfy sofas and armchairs – none of the ugly upright armchairs with their wooden arms you would usually see in an old folks' home. It was surprisingly homely.

Dickie Ledgard sprang to his feet when they entered. 'Mrs Gladwell! How are you? Have my seat, it's nice and warm here by the fire.' He ushered Iris into his armchair. 'Would you like tea, or coffee?'

'TEA WOULD BE GRAND.'

There was no sign of Violet Baxter, but Patricia Haddington was beside the trolley, in charge of the teapot. Max Plum was sitting in an armchair reading the *Daily Mail*, and Roger Darnton was standing by the French doors, looking out into the garden, ignoring everyone else. The other residents, about half a dozen or so, were dotted in groups around the table and sofas, some drinking tea and chatting, others just staring into space. Patricia poured them both a cup of tea, and offered up a plate of ginger biscuits. Iris took three.

'How are you all?' Liz asked Patricia. 'The last few days must have been quite a strain?'

Patricia nodded. She did look a bit drawn and tense. 'It was a terrible shock for everyone. And the police have been a nuisance. Asking questions they really...'

She broke off as Violet Baxter bustled into the room. She was with two other women, a young one with a ponytail and an older one in a trouser suit and trainers. The older woman had a sharp black bob. Liz's heart sank.

'Is everyone here?' asked DI Flint.

'Except Mr Pearson, who's at the dentist,' said Violet Baxter.

'We can catch up with him later.' Flint turned to address

the room, in a tone much slower and louder than her normal speaking voice. 'Good morning, everyone. I'm the senior officer in charge of the investigation into Mrs Bendelow's death.' Her gaze snagged on Liz. She frowned, but continued to speak. 'As you can see, I've brought one of my lab colleagues this morning to take a DNA sample from you all.'

The young woman with the ponytail sat at a side table and opened her medical bag.

'If you could all line up here, please,' continued Flint, still enunciating insultingly clearly. 'The process is entirely pain-less and won't take long...'

'Whoa there! Hold your horses,' said Patricia Haddington. 'Surely we're not suspects?'

'Not suspects, no,' said Flint. 'The samples are just to eliminate you from our investigation.'

'If we're not suspects, why do we need eliminating?' coun-tered Patricia. 'That makes no sense.'

'NO, IT DOESN'T.' As a non-resident, Iris wasn't likely to be included in the DNA collection, but that didn't mean she had nothing to say about it.

'Legally,' continued Patricia, 'we're not obliged to give a swab sample. We're not persons of interest. Nor have we been arrested.'

Flint stared at her. 'You sound very certain of that, Mrs...?'

'Haddington. Patricia Haddington. I'm a retired solicitor.'

'I see.' Flint smiled, with effort. 'Strictly speaking, of course, you don't have to give a sample. But surely there's no harm in giving one, if...'

'So, are you saying we don't have to do it?' asked Roger Darnton.

'If you don't have to do it, I'm bloody well not going to,' cut in Max Plum.

'Me neither,' said Dickie Ledgard, folding his arms in defiance.

'NOR ME.'

'Good for you, Mrs Gladwell.' Dickie nodded encouragement to Iris, who beamed at him. Everyone else had been watching the exchange. The few people who had started to queue obediently at the table now wandered off in search of something better to do.

Flint stared at them all in dismay. She was so used to being able to bully people that she clearly had no idea how to handle anyone who stood their ground. For a moment, Liz actually felt sorry for her. But only for a moment. Flint caught her eye and scowled. She marched over.

'I suppose I have you to thank for this geriatric rebellion?'

'I only called in to collect Clara's things. This has nothing to do with me.'

'Since when has that stopped you getting involved?'

'Thank you, Detective Flint,' Patricia said as she joined the fray. 'We can see how busy you are. Don't let us take up any more of your time.'

'Detective *Inspector* Flint,' corrected Flint. She turned on her heel. 'We're wasting our time here,' she snapped to Violet Baxter as she headed out. The young woman with the ponytail packed up her swab packs and hurried in her wake.

'Oh dear,' said Dickie. 'I think we've ruffled the detective's feathers.'

'The Detective *Inspector's* feathers.' Roger grinned sardonically.

'Do her good,' sniffed Patricia. 'You've got to watch people like that. If you give them an inch, they'll take a mile.' She pushed up her cardigan sleeves.

Liz stifled an exclamation.

Patricia looked at the deep scratches on her forearms as if she'd never seen them before. 'Brambles. They'll take over everything if you let them. A bit like uppity detectives.'

6

'Any news from the lab?' asked Liz.

Kevin eyed her as he finished his sandwich. 'About?'

'The tissue under Clara's fingernails.'

Kevin sighed. 'You're like a dog with a bone.' He looked at Nelson, who was watching them from his spot at Liz's feet. 'Sorry, boy, but she is.'

Nelson said nothing. The bump on his nose had gone, and he was his usual sanguine self. They were all taking lunch *al fresco* in their favourite shelter on the West Cliff, looking out across the grey expanse of the sea. Unusually, there was no wind, which made it feel quite warm for February, although their breath was still visible when they spoke.

Kevin examined his sausage roll. 'Tilly's put some kind of herb in this, hasn't she? Do you know what it is?'

'Stop trying to change the subject.'

'No, the results haven't come back yet.' He took a bite of his sausage roll and spoke around it. 'But there's no hurry.

There's no point having a DNA profile if we have nothing to compare it with.'

'Assuming whoever did it doesn't already have a police record.'

'Yes, assuming that.'

'So you think it was someone she knew?'

Kevin didn't answer, but gave her a sideways look. 'Flint wasn't happy she couldn't get samples from the residents. She's blaming you.'

Liz shrugged. 'Nothing new there, is there?' She poured some more tea from the flask into their plastic cups. 'You might want to take a look at Patricia Haddington.'

'The solicitor? Why?'

'She has some nasty scratches on her arms. Says she did it gardening, but who gardens in February? And it was Patricia who put her foot down about giving samples.'

'Okay. We'll take a look at her. Anything else?'

Liz smiled slyly. 'I thought you didn't want me to get involved?'

'It looks like that ship has sailed, doesn't it?'

'Did you know that Clara's brother went missing, back in the 80s? He killed himself, supposedly.'

'Supposedly?'

'They never found a body. But they did find his clothes on West Cliff beach, and so eventually the coroner ruled it accidental drowning.'

'I doubt that has anything to do with Clara being murdered thirty years later, do you?'

'Probably not. But I thought I'd mention it.'

Kevin raised an eyebrow. 'Anything else?'

'Not yet, no.'

Kevin noted the 'yet'. 'Will you please do me a favour, and at least *try* to keep out of Flint's way?'

Liz nodded. 'The last thing I want to do is make things

difficult for you.' There was a lengthy pause. Liz thought a change of subject might be in order. 'How's Anna?'

'Fine. She's studying for her exams – the last qualification she needs before she can do a post mortem without supervision. What with that and this new investigation, we're not really managing to see a lot of each other.'

Liz frowned. It seemed that everyone's love life was in the doldrums.

Kevin perked up. 'I got her a Lucky Duck, by the way. I think she'll like it. And I've ordered flowers. A "romantic luxury bouquet".' He made speech marks in the air as he said it.

'Perfect.' She finished her own sausage roll. 'Have you had enough to eat?'

'Stuffed, thanks.'

'Good.' Liz started to pack their things away. 'I'll take Iris the rest of these sandwiches.'

'How is she?'

'Hard to tell. You know what she's like, Dunkirk spirit and all that. I'm sure she'd appreciate a visit sometime, if you can manage it?'

Kevin looked at his watch. 'I can give you a lift over there now, if you like? Pop in for a couple of minutes?'

'Sounds good.'

Liz had thought Iris would be pleased to see Kevin, but if she was, she did an excellent job of hiding it. She glared at them both when she opened the door.

'WHAT DO YOU TWO WANT?'

Her face was pink and puffy. Liz wondered if the old lady had been crying. Kevin darted Liz a look of concern.

'We've brought you some lunch,' said Liz.

'I SUPPOSE YOU'D BETTER COME IN THEN.' Iris

stomped off inside, leaving them to follow her into the kitchen. Liz tried not to stare. Benbow Cottage, never a contender for home of the year, now looked like someone had tossed a hand grenade into it. The table was littered with photographs and papers. Clara's boxes were empty on the floor, beside heaps of clothes and random scattered ornaments. The countertops were cluttered with empty tins and dirty dishes, and the sink was overflowing,

'YOU'LL WANT TEA, DO YOU?' barked Iris.

Kevin shook his head. 'Not for me, thanks, I've got to get back to the station.'

'I'm fine, too,' said Liz. 'I'll just give you these sandwiches and be on my way.'

'How are you, Iris?' asked Kevin.

Iris glared. 'WHY DO PEOPLE KEEP ASKING ME THAT? I'M FINE. WHY WOULDN'T I BE?' She took the foil-wrapped package from Liz. 'WHY WOULDN'T I BE? I'M PERFECTLY FINE.'

'There's sausage rolls in there, too,' soothed Liz. 'I know you like them.'

'I'M FINE.'

Iris turned away to put the package in her ancient fridge. While her back was turned, Liz and Kevin had an urgent, silent conversation. Kevin's eyes were wide: *What shall we do?* Liz grimaced and jerked her head in the direction of the door: *You go. I'll deal with it.*

Kevin sidled to the door. 'Sorry, I have to get back to work, Iris,' he said. 'I'll pop in again later, shall I?'

'WHATEVER.' Iris waved her hand dismissively. 'PLEASE YOURSELF.' She looked at Liz. 'WHAT ABOUT YOU?'

'Actually, I've changed my mind. I'd love a cup of tea.'

Iris harrumphed.

Kevin made his escape, with one last worried glance at Liz.

Iris busied herself trying to find clean cups and the teapot among the mess. Liz sat at the table, and pushed some of the photographs aside to give her elbow room. There must have been more than a hundred – most of them were black and white, although there were a few more modern colour ones, and also some faded Polaroids from the 70s and 80s. Curious, Liz looked through them. The majority were of people in formal clothes standing stiffly for the camera. There were some of Clara posing at the Tower of London, Big Ben and Covent Garden. Others showed her in Whitby, standing on the pier, or sitting on the beach. One particular black and white photo caught Liz's eye. She picked it up.

It was of two young girls, sitting in a boat. From the leafy island behind them, and the oriental lanterns strung through the trees, Liz recognised the boating lake at Peasholm Park in Scarborough. One of the girls was Clara, decades younger, but still recognisable. She was holding onto her straw hat and laughing. The other girl, wearing a 60s-style polka dot dress, was also laughing. Liz peered at her more closely.

'Iris?'

'WHAT?' Iris turned, a teabag in each hand.

Liz held up the photograph. 'This is you, isn't it? In this photo?'

Iris blinked.

'I thought you said you hadn't known Clara long?'

'I DON'T KNOW WHY I SAID THAT...I PANICKED.'

'Why on earth would you panic?'

Iris hesitated. 'ME AND CLARA WERE WORKING UNDERCOVER.'

'What?'

'WE WERE ON THE TRAIL OF A MURDERER.'

'A murderer?'

'AND A FRAUD AND LIAR.'

Liz's head was spinning. 'Who? Why?'

'SO MANY QUESTIONS!'

'Well... yes.'

'LET ME MAKE THIS TEA. THEN I'LL TELL YOU EVERYTHING.'

Two minutes later, Iris joined Liz at the table and handed her a steaming mug of tea. She picked up the photograph of herself and Clara and looked at it sadly.

'I REMEMBER THIS LIKE IT WAS YESTERDAY. EDDIE TOOK IT.'

Liz tried to remember where she'd heard that name before. 'Clara's brother?'

Iris nodded. 'HE ALMOST FELL IN THE BOATING LAKE. I WAS LAUGHING SO HARD I THOUGHT I WAS GOING TO WET MYSELF.' She scowled. 'EDDIE DIDN'T KILL HIMSELF. HE WOULD NEVER HAVE DONE SOME-THING LIKE THAT.'

'But the coroner said...'

'BUGGER THE CORONER. HE DIDN'T KNOW WHAT HE WAS TALKING ABOUT. EDDIE WAS MURDERED.'

'By...?'

'ROGER DARNTON.'

Liz frowned. 'Okay. I'm getting quite confused here. Perhaps you'd better start at the beginning?'

Iris settled more comfortably into her chair and took a deep breath.

'DARNTON WAS A MEDIUM – USED TO DO SHOWS AT SCARBOROUGH AND FILEY, BACK IN THE 80s. THEN, WHEN HE TURNED UP AT THE ANCHORAGE A FEW WEEKS AGO, HE DIDN'T RECOGNISE CLARA, BUT SHE RECOGNISED HIM. I AGREED TO HELP HER GET HER REVENGE.'

'Because he killed Eddie?'

'EXACTLY.'

'Why would he kill Eddie?'

'HE AND EDDIE FELL OUT ABOUT SOMETHING – I DON'T KNOW WHAT. EDDIE JOINED THE SCEPTICS SOCIETY, DETERMINED TO UNMASK HIM. HE FOUND OUT DARNTON WAS CONNING PEOPLE. NOT JUST CONNING THEM, BUT BLACKMAILING THEM, TOO.'

'He wasn't really a medium?' The question was out before Liz realised the absurdity of it. As far as she was concerned, all mediums were fakes. Or self-deluded.

'NO. HE WAS A COMMON OR GARDEN CRIMINAL. EDDIE REPORTED HIM TO THE POLICE AND THEY LOCKED HIM UP.'

'I don't understand. If Darnton was in prison, how did he kill Eddie?'

'HE WAS OUT ON BAIL WHEN EDDIE WENT MISS-ING. CLARA AND I ALWAYS THOUGHT HE'D HAD A HAND IN IT.'

It dawned on Liz. 'So the Ouija board was a set up?'

'IT WAS CLARA'S IDEA. SHE BELIEVED IN THAT KIND OF THING, AND THOUGHT IT WAS THE PERFECT WAY TO GET DARNTON TO CRACK, TO ADMIT WHAT HE'D DONE.' Iris wiped a tear from her eye. 'IT DIDN'T WORK, BUT WE MUST HAVE SPOOKED HIM. HE MUST HAVE REALISED CLARA WAS PUSHING THAT PLANCHETTE THINGY.'

'You think he killed her?'

'OF COURSE HE DID! BUT I DON'T KNOW HOW TO PROVE IT.' She looked pleadingly at Liz. 'CAN YOU HELP ME?'

7

'Take a deep breath, everyone,' instructed Doctor Darke. 'What can you smell?'

'The sea?' suggested a middle-aged lady.

'Fish and chips!' called a young girl, in the company of her mum, dad and younger sister.

'My farts!' shouted Lukasz Polonsky, who was there with his twin brother Eryk and his mum Gryzna. Gryzna shot him a warning look, but she needn't have worried. The doctor wasn't put off his stride – he was used to the twins' high spirits.

'Are you sure that's all? Are you sure you can't smell the faintest whiff of...' he paused dramatically, 'burning?'

Everyone sniffed again. Their little group of tourists was gathered in the claustrophobically narrow alleyway of Ellerby Lane, which ran between Church Street and Sandgate. Even though it was just five o'clock in the afternoon, it was dark. The lane was lit only by neighbouring cottage windows and a single streetlamp. It was very spooky.

Doctor Darke – aka Niall – sniffed the air extravagantly. He was wearing his top hat, and the crimson cape that Liz had made for Tilly at Halloween. His face was gaunt with white and grey stage make-up.

'Oh!' exclaimed the middle-aged lady. 'I think I can, a bit. Can you smell it, Mum?'

The old lady next to her nodded. 'I can.'

Liz stifled a smile and exchanged a look with the statuesque Gryzna, who was clearly thinking the same thing: People were so gullible. Liz had to admit, however, that Niall was very compelling. In the two hours since they'd started, he'd led them down countless streets and alleyways and told a myriad of tales: of ghostly monks, one-armed lighthouse keepers, witches, and a phantom funeral coach pulled by headless horses. At the bottom of the abbey steps, he'd told the story of Constance de Beverley, a nun who broke her vows of chastity and was supposedly bricked up alive in the abbey walls, and he had also described how Dracula, disguised as a black dog, had bounded up the steps after the wreck of the *Demeter*. At that point, even Liz had had to suppress a shiver. She'd had a close personal encounter with the town's famous demon dog – the Barguest – at Halloween. Even though it had ultimately turned out to be something else altogether, the memory of its burning yellow eyes still sent a thrill of horror through her.

Now they were on the final leg of their journey. Doctor Darke turned to the children in the group.

'Can any of you young people tell me where we get bread from?'

'The Co-op!' piped Eryk.

'Would you believe,' said Niall, 'that in the days before our marvellous supermarkets, people used to bake bread themselves?'

The children looked sceptical.

'But... many people in Whitby were too poor to have their own ovens, so, for a small fee, the local baker used to let people bake their bread and warm up their dinners in his oven. Remember we saw the old Bakehouse, in Bakehouse Yard?'

Everyone nodded.

'One day, a customer came into the bakery – little Mary Clarke, only ten years old. The baker knew her well – she often came to heat up her father's dinners there – and he let her put her pot in the oven herself. His back had only been turned for a second when he heard a blood-curdling scream.'

The old lady gasped.

Doctor Darke continued with relish, knowing he had his audience in the palm of his hand. 'The baker was horrified to see Mary engulfed in flames. Her beautiful long hair had been set alight by sparks from the oven. Unsure what to do, he tried to beat the flames out. But Mary ran. She ran out of Bakehouse Yard, and down this very lane where we're standing, towards the infirmary on Grape Lane.'

Everyone looked around the alleyway where they were standing, with a new and horrified perspective.

'But when she got there,' said Niall, 'it was too late. There was nothing they could do to save her.'

Liz had heard the same tale told by locals, but with grislier details. She guessed that Niall had watered it down for the two little girls. He wouldn't have been worried about Lukasz and Eryk – the gorier the better, as far as they were concerned.

Niall finished the story. 'Some people say that if you walk down this lane and you smell burning, it's a sure sign that little Mary's ghost is about to appear. She'll run through you, silently screaming, with her hair in flames.'

Everyone was silent.

'I don't like that story,' said one of the little girls, fiddling nervously with her plait.

'Don't you?' Niall bent to talk to her, his Irishness

temporarily leaking through the modulated tones of Doctor
Darke. 'Sure, don't you worry about that. I have another story.
This one is about puppets. Do you like puppets?'

The girl nodded, although to Liz's eyes she looked less
than convinced.

Niall stood up again and flourished his cape. 'Then follow
me, fellow thrill-seekers, back to the place we began our journey! That is also our final destination.'

They returned to the old town hall in the market square,
with its columns and clock tower. Once there, Niall told his
final tale, of a puppeteer driven to murder by a drunken
heckler. He then accepted payment from his audience. He
tried to refuse Gryzna's money, but she insisted. She said
good night to them both, then led the boys away, ignoring
their noisy pleas for chips.

'Well?' said Niall, when everyone else had gone. 'What
did you think?' He looked exhilarated.

'You were marvellous.'

'Really?'

'Oscar-worthy. I've heard some of the stories before, but it
was like I was hearing them for the first time.'

'It was even more fun than I thought it would be.' He
jingled the cash in his pocket. 'And the money's grand too,
thanks to the tips.'

'Well deserved.'

They headed down Church Street towards home. All the
shops were closed, and the street was virtually deserted. Now
that the Christmas decorations were down, it was probably
the bleakest time of year in the town. They were just passing
the Museum of Whitby Jet and the entrance to New Way
Ghaut when they saw a young woman sitting on the pavement, her face illuminated by her phone. At first Liz thought
there was somebody with her, but then she realised it was a
giant rucksack leaning against the wall beside her.

As they got closer they heard the girl sigh.

'Are you okay?' asked Liz. 'Are you lost?'

She looked up at them. She had big eyes, strong cheekbones and her hair braided on the top of her head. There was something sturdy and Germanic about her, like a Rhinemaiden or a Valkyrie.

'Not according to my sat nav,' she said. 'It says I have "reached my destination". But I can't find it anywhere.'

Niall grinned down at her. 'Sure, sat nav's worse than useless around here.'

The girl looked startled. Niall remembered how he was dressed, and took off his top hat. 'Where is it you're looking for?'

'Neptune Yard.'

Niall nodded. 'It's literally a minute away, but you'd never find it if you didn't know it was there.'

Liz smiled at the girl. 'We're going that way. We'll take you, if you like?'

'That would be brilliant, thanks.' The girl scrambled to her feet and dusted off her jeans.

Niall pointed at her rucksack. 'Can I give you a hand with that?'

'I'm fine.' She swung the big rucksack expertly up onto her shoulders. 'I'm used to lugging this brute around.'

They started walking.

'Fancy dress party, is it?' the girl asked Niall.

'Ah no, not exactly. It's work.'

The girl opened her eyes wide. 'You'll be doing the graveyard shift, then?' They both grinned at each other.

'Where exactly in Neptune Yard are you going?' asked Liz.

'Benbow Cottage.'

Niall stopped walking. 'Iris?'

'Iris Gladwell, yes.'

It dawned on Liz who she was. 'Are you Clara Bendelow's niece?'

'Leah Bendelow.'

'I'm Liz, and this is Niall.'

They all shook hands.

'Pleased to meet you,' said Leah. 'Did you both know Clara?'

Niall shook his head.

'I only met her once,' said Liz. 'Just before...' she broke off, not knowing how to finish that sentence.

'I didn't really know her, either,' said Leah. 'I think I met her once when I was a little girl. I didn't really know who she was, and hadn't realised she was all alone up here.'

Liz realised Leah was shivering, and wondered how long she had been wandering around Whitby in the cold.

'Let's not stand around here chattering,' she said. 'Let's get you to Iris.'

'HERE YOU ARE.' Iris clattered a bowl of stew in front of Leah. 'GET THAT DOWN YOU. IT'LL WARM YOU RIGHT UP.'

'Thanks.'

'You managed to get back from Nepal very quickly,' said Liz.

Leah nodded. 'I was already in Kathmandu when I got the call from the police. I just brought my flight home forward a few days.'

'What's it like?' asked Niall. 'Nepal? I've always wanted to go there.'

'Breath-taking. Metaphorically and literally – the altitude takes a bit of getting used to. But the landscape is wonderful, and the people are the friendliest in the world.'

'HOW'S THAT STEW?'

'Delicious, thanks. You're all so lovely.'

To Liz's surprise, Niall blushed, red cheeks visible even through his make-up.

She stifled a smile. 'I assume the police gave you this address?'

Leah nodded. 'They said that Iris was acting as Clara's next of kin. I'm so glad she had such lovely friends.'

They all watched her eat in silence for a moment or two, until Liz asked the question they were all thinking.

'How much did the police tell you?'

'FOR HEAVEN'S SAKE,' snapped Iris. 'LET THE POOR LASS GET HER DINNER IN PEACE. YOU'LL GIVE HER INDIGESTION.'

'It's okay,' said Leah. 'I don't mind, honestly.' She spooned up her stew. 'They didn't tell me much, just that auntie was dead, under suspicious circumstances, and they were investigating. They gave me a contact to call when I got here.' She fished a piece of paper out of her jeans pocket, and read it out. 'DI Fiona Flint. It's probably too late to call her now, isn't it? I'll do it in the morning.' Leah looked at them. 'Do you know what happened?'

Liz pulled a face. 'Not really.' It was better that Leah should get her information from the police.

'Where are you staying tonight?' asked Niall, by way of changing the subject.

'I don't know. I've been in such a rush to get here I didn't think to book anywhere. Is there a hotel or something nearby?'

Liz felt bad at not being able to offer a bed. Kipper had Helen and Andrew staying in it, and there was no room in Gull with her and Niall. And most of the accommodation in the town wasn't available on a nightly basis.

'There's the Esplanade. Or Bagdale Hall,' suggested Niall.

'As long as you don't mind the ghost.' He caught Liz's expression. 'The pirate, Browne Bushall.'

'DON'T BE DAFT,' bellowed Iris. 'YOU CAN STAY HERE. I'LL MAKE UP THE BED IN THE SPARE ROOM.'

Liz wasn't sure that was the best idea. The cottage was even more chaotic than it had been when she was last there. But Leah didn't seem to mind.

'Oh, that would be lovely. Are you sure? I don't want to put you to any bother.'

'NO BOTHER AT ALL. IT'LL BE NICE HAVING THE COMPANY.'

After Leah had finished her stew, and Liz had made sure Iris had all the bedding she needed, Liz and Niall said goodnight. They walked the hundred metres or so to Gull Cottage in thoughtful silence.

'It'll be good for Iris to have someone there,' said Liz, as they let themselves in.

'It will,' agreed Niall. He bent to pat Nelson, who came to greet them.

'Leah seems nice, doesn't she?' Liz glanced at him with a mischievous expression.

'She does.' Niall grinned. 'Very, very nice.'

8

A s Liz got dressed the next morning, she found herself thinking about Clara Bendelow. Clara had spent her old age alone, with no family to visit her, or really care whether she lived or died. It was a sobering thought. Liz didn't want to indulge in self-pity, but she knew the same thing could very well happen to her. She and Mark hadn't been able to have children, thanks to a nasty dose of mumps Mark had had when he was a teenager, that left him infertile. They had briefly thought about adopting, but then decided against it. They had each other, and that was the important thing.

And now, here she was, a widow.

Liz gave herself a mental shake as she went to the dressing table. There were plenty of people who had children, and still died alone and unloved. And, strictly speaking, she *did* have family – her sister, Julie. But, like Leah, Julie had the wanderlust. Liz had no idea what continent she might be on at any given time. The infrequent postcards she received were usually weeks or even months out of date.

Liz also couldn't deny that she'd made some very good

friends since coming to Whitby – Tilly and Mags, Kevin and Benedict, Iris and Irwin, and Gryzna and her boys. And Niall, of course. In some ways, Niall felt like the son she'd never had, but Liz knew she had to be careful there. Niall had a loving mother in Dublin, and nobody needed *two* mothers, did they? She had to make a conscious effort to rein in her protective urges where Niall was concerned.

Liz pushed one of her ruby studs through her ear, and then looked for the other one. It didn't seem to be in the little tray on the dresser where she kept her day-to-day jewellery. She tipped the tray out onto the bed to make sure. But no, it wasn't there.

She couldn't remember taking the studs out the last time she'd worn them. Had one accidentally fallen on the floor? She got on her knees to look, but all she found were dust bunnies under the bed. She got to her feet again, ignoring the evidence of her shoddy housekeeping. Had she lost the earring somewhere outside? The possibility made her eyes prickle. She didn't want to lose one of Mark's last gifts. Liz dismissed the thought. Surely she'd have noticed when she'd taken them out? If she was careful with the Hoover, it would probably turn up.

She went downstairs, her thoughts turning back to Clara. Iris was convinced that Roger Darnton had killed Eddie Bendelow. But that seemed far-fetched. If Roger had killed him, what had he done with the body? Had he taken it out to sea in a boat? Or dumped it somewhere else? And why? Because Eddie had exposed him as a fraud? It all seemed a bit extreme and unlikely.

After taking Nelson out for his morning walk and seeing Niall off to work, Liz settled herself down at her laptop to do some online sleuthing. First, she searched Roger Darnton. She found some publicity photographs of him, taken when he was doing the séance circuit in the late 80s. The man in the photographs, who always had a cigarette in his hand, was younger, but it was definitely Roger Darnton. It must have been a terrible shock for Clara to recognise him after so many years.

Apart from the photographs, Liz couldn't find anything else about Darnton, not even anything about his conviction. She guessed she would probably have to look in the archives at the *Whitby Bugle* for that.

Then Liz searched for spiritualist groups in the area. Darnton had seemed keen to join in the séance at the Anchorage. In Liz's experience, a leopard rarely changed its spots, so perhaps he would be involved with a local spiritualist group? There were quite a few in North Yorkshire, mostly Spiritualist Churches, but only one group based in Whitby – the Third Eye Society, run by medium Hilda Blakey. That might be an avenue worth pursuing.

Lastly, she searched for the North Yorkshire Sceptics Society. Iris had said that Eddie had joined the sceptics to expose Roger Darnton. Even though that was a long time ago, it still might be worth looking into. According to their website, the sceptics met in the Esplanade Hotel once a month. Their stated aim was '*the application of reason to any and all ideas. To demand compelling evidence before accepting any thing as truth.*'

Sounded sensible. Liz scanned the list of trustees, and stopped abruptly. The group's treasurer was a name she knew. At first, she was surprised, but, after further thought, she realised she shouldn't be surprised at all.

DORA SPACKLE WAS Head Curator of the Abbey Museum that sat on the clifftop beside St Mary's church and the abbey ruins. It was housed in a huge Georgian mansion that had been cleverly restored and adapted to display exhibits, and to serve as the ticket office and entrance into the abbey itself.

Liz waited by the museum gates, knowing that Dora usually ate her lunch in her car. If she'd been trying to meet anyone else, Liz would have brought Nelson along for a clifftop walk, but Nelson and Dora had a long-running feud. It had started after an incident involving one of Dora's handbags and a vicious kick that had – thankfully – missed Nelson by a whisker. Now Nelson growled whenever he heard Dora's name, and went into paroxysms whenever he saw her. Liz couldn't really blame him.

At one minute past one, Liz saw a figure emerge from the museum and head across the formal garden towards the car park. She was wearing a tweed coat and her habitual cloche hat, and her spectacles glinted in the winter sunlight. As Dora got nearer, Liz saw her stiffen. She lifted her chin and marched right past without even acknowledging her.

'Dora,' called Liz. 'Could I have a word?'

Dora didn't slow her march towards her red Mini Clubman. 'About what?'

'The Sceptics Society.'

Dora stopped and turned towards her in horror. 'You're not wanting to join, are you?'

'No.'

'Good. We do have standards, you know.'

Liz ignored the barb. 'I was wondering how long you've been involved with the society?'

'Why? What is it to you?'

'I'm asking because of Clara Bendelow.'

Dora's expression softened a little. 'Poor Mrs Bendelow.'

'Did you know her?'

'Of course I did. We both lived here all our lives.' Dora sniffed. 'Unlike some people. Moving here and thinking they own the place.'

Another barb that Liz ignored. 'Did you know her brother Eddie?'

Dora's eyes narrowed. 'You can't help yourself, can you? One sniff of tragedy and you have to poke your nose in.'

'It's not like that at all.' Liz was hurt. 'Clara was a friend of Iris's. A good friend. I just want to help if I can.'

'If you say so.'

Liz ploughed on. 'Eddie was a member of the Sceptics Society. I heard that he helped the society uncover a fake medium.'

Dora snorted. 'All mediums are fake.'

'I wouldn't argue with that. But I was wondering if you remember anything about it? It was in the late 80s, I think. The medium was Roger Darnton.'

'I wasn't involved with the society then. I was just a slip of a thing, barely out of school.'

Liz tried not to let her own scepticism show. Dora was in her mid-fifties at least.

'But I do remember it,' continued Dora. 'There was a court case, wasn't there?'

'Yes. Darnton went to prison.'

'I'm glad to hear it. There are far too many frauds and charlatans about. Hilda Blakey, for one. And that Rose Young on the pier.'

Liz knew Dora was talking about Hilda Blakey of the Third Eye Society, but she had no idea who Rose Young might be. She thought it best not to encourage Dora to rake over her personal prejudices, and steered her back to the point.

'I was wondering whether the society might have any records I could take a look at?'

'I shouldn't think so. That was years ago. Even if we had, I wouldn't let you rummage through them. If you take my advice, you'll stop poking your nose into other people's business.' Dora peered at Liz. 'You do know it makes you unpopular, don't you?'

Liz was speechless. *Was* she unpopular? She didn't think so. And at least *she* didn't have to sit in her car and eat lunch on her own! Luckily, Dora cut in again before Liz had the chance to voice what she was thinking.

'I have to get on. I only get half an hour for lunch, and you're wasting it.'

WHEN SHE GOT HOME, Liz called the number on the Third Eye Society website. It rang a few times before someone picked up.

'Good afternoon. Hilda Blakey speaking.'

'Hello.' Liz cleared her throat. 'Is this the Third Eye Society?'

'Indeed it is. I sense you have a question for me?'

Well, yes, of course she had. Otherwise she wouldn't be ringing, would she?

'Roger Darnton recommended I get in touch with you. He said you could help me.' That was a gamble, but going on her hunch that a leopard doesn't change its spots, she thought it was one worth taking. If Roger hadn't had any contact with the society, there was no reason to take the conversation any further.

'Ah. Yes,' said Hilda Blakey. 'Mr Darnton is one of our newer members. And gifted... quite gifted, himself. Is there someone on the other side you are particularly wanting to reach out to?'

The question caught Liz off guard. She answered without thinking: 'My husband'.

'And when did he pass into the spirit realm?'

'Five years ago.' Liz could have kicked herself. She really didn't want to dishonour Mark's memory by involving him in silly hocus-pocus.

'It may well be that he has moved on already. But we shall

certainly try our best to reach out to him for you. We're having one of our regular séances on Wednesday night. Why don't you come along? And bring something that belonged to your husband, so we can make a strong connection.'

'You're going to a *what*?' asked Benedict.

'A séance.'

'Oh, can I come?' Tilly clapped her hands. 'I've always wanted to go to one.' Tilly and Mags were into anything spiritual. Their shop in the café sold all kinds of new age items, such as tarot cards, crystals and spiritual self-help books.

'Maybe next time,' said Liz. 'I don't want to just turn up with you uninvited.'

Tilly looked disappointed.

'What exactly are you trying to find out?' asked Benedict. He seemed distracted, toying with his cheese and onion toastie rather than eating it. Liz had been surprised to see him. She knew he occasionally had lunch in the café, but hadn't seen him there for weeks. His question was a good one. Why exactly was she going to the Third Eye Society séance?

'I'm not entirely sure,' she said. 'I suppose I want to find out what kind of man Roger Darnton is. Iris is convinced he killed Eddie Bendelow and now Clara.'

'Have you told Kevin about that yet?' asked Tilly.

Liz shook her head.

'Perhaps you should,' said Benedict. 'Not that it's likely to have anything to do with Clara's death, but it should at least be on police radar.'

Liz nodded. He was probably right.

'Who was it you told Mrs Blakey you're trying to contact?' asked Tilly.

Liz hesitated. 'Mark.'

Benedict and Tilly both stared at her. She hardly ever mentioned Mark to them, much less to a total stranger.

'Is that a good idea?' asked Benedict. 'Isn't it just going to stir things up again?'

'What things?' said Tilly.

'Grief.' Benedict knew what he was talking about. His own wife Katherine had died just over twelve months before.

'I wish I hadn't mentioned him,' said Liz. 'But she caught me off guard. I'm supposed to take something that belonged to him.'

'Really?' said Benedict. From his expression it was clear he was liking the situation less and less.

'There's no way I'm going to do that, obviously,' said Liz. 'I'll have to think of something else to take.'

9

'I'm sensing that your departed husband was a fair bit younger than you?'

On the face of it, that was quite an impressive deduction, given the sock Hilda was clutching belonged to Niall. Slightly less so when you knew it had a winking emoji on it.

Liz just nodded.

'Okay everyone, let's make a start. Graham, can you close the blinds, please?'

There were another four people attending the session: Roger Darnton and three others who hadn't introduced themselves – a middle-aged couple and a young woman who refused to take off her coat, even though the room was sweltering. Hilda ushered everyone to a chair around the circular table in the middle of the room, while her husband Graham – a tall, balding man with a beard and a pale complexion – closed the venetian blinds.

The room surprised Liz. It was clearly Hilda's dining room, and there had been no effort made to spooky it up. No curtains, no crystal ball, no tablecloth. It was all disappointingly ordinary. Graham removed the arrangement of dried flowers from the centre of the table and dimmed the lights slightly.

'Is everyone comfortable?' asked Hilda. Liz had half expected her to appear in a turban and kaftan, but she was wearing a pale blue fluffy sweater and jeans. She was quite an odd-looking woman, with silver hair and small, almost black eyes. Combined with her thick glasses, they gave her the air of a small woodland mammal. She peered at Liz.

'Are you comfortable, Mrs McLuckie?'

'Yes, thank you.'

'We'll start with a prayer.'

Everyone put their hands together and closed their eyes.

'Dear Lord,' murmured Hilda, 'we pray for your protection as we begin this practice. You are our keeper...'

Liz opened one eye and peeped around the table. Everyone had their eyes closed, except Roger Darnton – who, she was alarmed to see, was staring directly at her. She squeezed her eye shut again.

Hilda continued: 'Protect us from those who would harm us. Guard our going out and our going in, from this time and forever. In Jesus's name, Amen.'

'Amen,' echoed everyone. They all opened their eyes.

'Let us join hands,' said Hilda.

They all joined hands around the table. Liz was sitting between Graham and the young woman, whose fingers were slick with sweat. Liz looked at her in concern. Her narrow face was very pale.

Someone moaned.

Liz's attention snapped back to Hilda, who now had her eyes closed again, and her mouth slightly open. She moaned again, then took a deep breath in.

'I am in contact,' she said.

That was fast!

Hilda took some more deep breaths, and swayed from side to side. 'I am in contact with a woman. I can feel a restriction around my chest. I can't breathe. This lady had lung problems in life.'

Liz looked around the table. Roger was watching Hilda closely, while the middle-aged couple were clutching each other's hands and staring at her. Not all eyes were on the medium, however. Liz saw that Graham was watching the young woman beside her, who had gone even paler than before.

Hilda swayed. 'The lady's name begins with a J. Jill? No, not Jill... Jane.'

The young woman gripped Liz's fingers so tightly she almost yelped.

'Definitely Jane,' said Hilda with a nod.

'Mam?' The word came from the young woman as a strangled whisper.

Liz felt a surge of anger on her behalf.

'She has a message,' said Hilda. Her voice changed. 'You don't need to worry about me any more, pet. I have no more pain.' They were spoken in a Geordie accent – a not-very-convincing Geordie accent, in Liz's opinion – but they had the desired effect.

The young woman's fingers slipped from Liz's grasp, and there was a crash. Everyone was about to leap up, when Graham spoke urgently.

'Please! Stay where you are. It's dangerous to bring my wife out of the trance too fast.'

Everyone had to ignore the stricken girl on the floor, as Graham spoke soothingly to his wife.

'Hilda. Come back to us, love.'

Hilda opened her eyes slowly, and looked around as if she'd forgotten where she was. Graham looked relieved.

'What happened?' asked Hilda.

'Miss Fairlie's fainted.'

'Oh dear. Is she alright?'

At Graham's signal, everyone hurried to pick up the young woman. She looked around with a dazed expression as they propped her back in her chair.

'Tea, Graham, I think,' said Hilda, briskly.

Graham bustled into the kitchen, followed by the other two men. Liz watched the older women try to revive the younger one.

'There, there, dear,' soothed Hilda, rubbing her hands.

'Sorry. I feel such an idiot.' It was the first time Liz had heard the young woman speak, but wasn't surprised that she had a pronounced Geordie accent.

'Please don't worry about it,' said Hilda. 'It's a perfectly natural reaction. It can be very disconcerting, having your first contact with the other side.'

'Are your meetings always like this?' asked the other woman. It was clearly her first visit too, and she seemed more than a little awed by the proceedings.

Liz wasn't impressed. In fact, she was infuriated. Not wanting to give her feelings away, she wandered into the kitchen, where Graham and the middle-aged man were fussing over mugs and the kettle. The back door was open. Liz kept going, into the back yard.

Roger Darnton was already there, smoking a cigarette in the darkness. The tip of his cigarette glowed as took a deep drag on it. He blew the smoke into the frosty air.

'Bunch of amateurs,' he said. He looked at her speculatively. 'Did you know there was a man standing behind you the whole time in there? Even before we started the session. Hilda couldn't see him.'

Liz bit her lip. It was common knowledge in the town that she was a widow.

'I don't believe in ghosts,' she said.

'So why are you here? Hilda tells me I recommended her to you, but we both know that's not true.' He looked at her with shrewd eyes. 'What kind of game are you playing, Mrs McLuckie?'

'I don't know what you mean.'

'There was also that silly business with the Ouija board at the Anchorage. Quite the performance. Do you take me for a fool?'

Liz couldn't think of anything to say. She was beginning to suspect he was a lot of things, but a fool wasn't one of them.

Seeing he wasn't going to get an answer to his question, he grinned sardonically. 'If I were you, I'd watch my step.' He flicked his cigarette into the bushes. 'You know what they say about curiosity, don't you?' He turned and went back into the kitchen.

After a minute or two, Liz followed him.

She found everyone drinking tea in the dining room.

'Care for a cuppa, Mrs McLuckie?' offered Graham.

'No, thank you.'

'I think we'll end our session after this,' said Hilda. 'I'm quite worn out, and I think everyone else has had enough for one night, don't you?'

Liz certainly had. Her objective had been to find out what kind of a man Roger Darnton was, and now she had her answer.

They ended with another prayer, and then headed out into the night. As they went up the garden path, Liz saw there was a small group of people waiting for them on the pavement. She recognised one of the shorter ones by the cloche hat she was wearing.

Dora thrust something at Roger, who was the first out of the gate. It looked like a leaflet.

'Read this,' she urged. 'Educate yourself.'

Roger crumpled it up and dropped it on the pavement.

Dora scurried to pick it up. Someone else thrust a leaflet at the middle-aged couple, who hurried to get past them as quickly as possible. The young woman burst through the cordon and practically ran to her car.

'You're deluding yourself!' Dora called after her, then she spotted Liz and her eyes widened.

'Evening, Dora.'

Dora thrust a leaflet at her. It was dark, but Liz could still read the headline. '*Is there life after death? A scientific viewpoint.*'

'What are you doing there?' shouted Hilda from the doorway. 'Is that you, Dora Spackle? This is private property!'

'We're not on your property!' Dora shouted back. 'We're on the public highway.'

'This is harassment. I'll call the police! Graham, go and call the police.'

Liz hurried away. The last thing she wanted was to be involved in a public disturbance. She could imagine what Detective Inspector Flint would have to say about that! As she got to the end of the street she looked back. She could see the knot of people at the gate, and hear voices raised. She put on a burst of speed to get round the corner.

She walked home thoughtfully. Although no one had asked her for money, it was pretty obvious Hilda Blakey was exploiting her clients for gain. She'd seen the middle-aged man and the young woman press bank notes into Graham's hand as they left. It infuriated her that the grandiosely named Third Eye Society was feeding on people's grief. As for Roger, Liz wasn't sure exactly what his game was, or why he had involved himself with the society. But she did know one thing: He was dangerous.

10

'So, what do you think? Do you think he killed Clara?' Kevin wound spaghetti carefully around his fork, trying not to splash sauce on the tablecloth.

'I have no idea. I don't like Roger Darnton, but that doesn't mean he's a murderer,' said Liz. 'But Iris is adamant he killed Clara and Eddie Bendelow.'

'I'd say that was a stretch,' said Benedict. 'He only did five months in prison. It's hardly worth killing for.' He caught Liz's surprised look. 'I went to the *Bugle*. Looked through their archives. You're not the only one who can sleuth, you know.'

His amused gaze caught Liz's and held for a second. She bent to her plate, ostensibly to eat spaghetti, but actually to hide her surprise. It was the first time Benedict had involved himself in any of her investigations.

'I disagree.' Tilly waved her own fork for emphasis. Liz had to make an effort to remember what it was that Tilly was disagreeing with. 'You have no idea what goes on in people's heads. You...' Tilly prodded her fork at Benedict, 'might not think five months in prison is worth killing for, but you're not a psychopath, are you?'

'Not as far as I know.' Benedict grinned. 'But do psychopaths actually know they're psychopaths?'

Liz tried not to stare at him. After being so reserved – withdrawn, even – for weeks, he now seemed to be back to his usual easy-going self. He and Liz had prepared the pre-Mah-jong supper as usual in his big kitchen, and had chatted away just like they used to do, with no awkward moments. It was almost as if he'd come to a decision of some kind.

Kevin laughed. 'Good point.'

Again, Liz had to struggle to remember what they'd been talking about.

'Actually,' sniffed Tilly, 'I think we're getting off the point. What I was trying to say is that we don't know what the killer's motivations might be.'

'That's true,' agreed Liz.

Kevin nodded. 'I don't think we can rule Darnton out, but I don't think we can rule him in either.'

Not particularly helpful. Liz frowned. 'Did you find out anything about Patricia Haddington? Those scratches on her arms looked nasty.'

Kevin wiped his mouth on his serviette. 'Violet Baxter confirmed that Patricia had helped her clear some brambles from the car park the day before Clara died.'

'Oh.' Liz was disappointed. 'I take it there's nothing back from the lab yet?'

'Not yet. DNA sequencing can take weeks. And, like I said, there's no particular hurry, because we don't have a suspect.'

'We have Darnton,' said Tilly.

'We don't have any evidence. Certainly not enough to warrant getting a sample from him.'

'We don't have to ask, though, do we?' Tilly brightened. 'We could steal his toothbrush or something?'

Kevin gave her a stern look. 'This isn't a TV drama. That kind of messing about would undermine the police investigation. It might even invalidate a prosecution.'

'Yes, but surely...'

'No, Tills,' interrupted Kevin. 'Absolutely not. Get a grip.'

Tilly stuck her tongue out at him. The two had known each other since school, and in many ways were more like brother and sister than friends.

Liz sighed. They didn't seem any closer to catching Clara's murderer than they had been the day her body was discovered.

Benedict voiced her thoughts. 'We're going round in circles.' He pushed his plate away. 'Who wants to play Mahjong?'

They all cleared the table, and Liz and Tilly stacked the dishwasher while Benedict and Kevin set up the table for their game.

'Those are pretty earrings,' said Tilly. 'I haven't seen them before, have I?'

'They're just cheap ones. I bought them this morning. I'd usually wear my ruby studs with this top, the ones Mark bought me for Valentine's, but I've lost one. It'll turn up eventually.' Unless she'd lost it outside somewhere, but she didn't want to think about that.

'Talking about Valentine's,' said Tilly, with a conspiratorial air, 'Niall and Leah Bendelow were in the café this afternoon.'

'Oh?' Liz knew he had a day off from the museum, but had no idea how he'd spent it.

'He was showing her around the town. They looked very friendly.' Tilly's eyes widened meaningfully.

'Friendly?'

'So friendly that I saw them kiss!'

'Good for them.' Liz was pleased for them both. She was

pleased for herself, too, if it meant Niall wouldn't be moping around the cottage like a restless puppy.

'Ready!' called out Kevin from the conservatory. 'Who wants a whupping?'

In fact, it was Liz who did the whupping. She came out overall winner, something that had only happened a couple of times since they'd started their regular games.

'You're on fire tonight, Mrs McLuckie,' said Kevin, clearing away the tiles.

'Isn't she?' Benedict's eyes met Liz's and she blushed.

'It's those little grey cells of hers working overtime,' said Tilly.

Kevin looked at his watch. 'Argh! Got to go. I'm picking Anna up from work. I take it you two would like a lift?'

'Yes, please.'

'That would be nice.'

'So soon?' Benedict looked disappointed. 'Why don't you stay for a bit longer, Liz? Have another glass of wine?'

Liz's heart skipped in her chest. She glanced at Tilly, who very pointedly pretended she hadn't heard Benedict's exclusive invitation. Liz hesitated.

'I'll walk you home after,' said Benedict.

'Okay, then,' said Liz. 'If you're sure.'

'Night, Liz.' Tilly suppressed a smirk as she kissed her cheek. Kevin wasn't quite so discreet. He winked at her as they went out the door.

'Still happy with white?' asked Benedict.

Liz nodded and he refilled her wine glass.

'Let's go through to the sitting room.'

The sitting room was lovely, a well-blended mix of Georgian architecture and modern, comfortable furniture. There was a fire crackling in the hob grate. Very romantic. Liz sat on one of the sofas, clutching her wine glass so hard her knuckles were white. Benedict arranged his long limbs in an armchair.

'I'm glad you decided to stay,' he said. 'I want to apologise to you.'

'For what?'

'I should have gone with you the other night. To that séance thing. It could have been dangerous.'

Liz shrugged. 'It could have been, I suppose, but it wasn't.'

'You have an awful habit of putting yourself in danger. You seem determined to give me a heart attack.'

Liz didn't know what to say to that. She took a gulp of wine instead. Benedict looked into the flames. 'It's funny, isn't it? How things change?'

'In what way?'

'Well... just over a year ago, I was sitting here with Kate. Now, here we are.'

'Yes.' Liz wondered where he was going with this.

'When she died, I thought my world had ended. I honestly did. But...the world keeps turning, doesn't it?'

Liz thought about Gillian Garraway, with whom he'd had a brief affair six months before. It seemed the world had turned pretty fast for him after Katherine's death. But then she pushed that uncharitable thought away. Loneliness was a terrible thing, and she wouldn't wish it on anyone.

'I felt the same way too,' she said, 'when Mark died. But now...'

'But now?' Benedict looked at her expectantly.

'I don't know... it's odd. In some ways, my life with him seems like yesterday, but it also feels like a lifetime ago. Like someone else's life.'

'Exactly!'

'I suppose it's nature's way of making it bearable. I'll always miss him, obviously, but... like you said, the world keeps turning.'

Benedict lifted his glass in a toast. 'To a turning world.'
Liz saluted him with hers. 'A turning world.'

11

'I SUPPOSE I'D BETTER GET SOME OF THIS STUFF TO CHARITY, NOW THAT LEAH HAS BEEN THROUGH IT.'

'Sorry, what?'

'ARE YOU OKAY?' Iris frowned at Liz. 'YOU LOOK A BIT PEAKY.'

'I'm fine.' She wasn't, though. She'd spent a sleepless night going over and over her conversation with Benedict in her head. He'd walked her home afterwards, and although they'd maintained a careful physical distance, when they reached Gull Cottage, he'd hesitated on the doorstep. She'd thought for one heart-stopping moment he was going to kiss her, but then the door had opened, making them both jump. It was Niall, with Nelson on his lead for his night-time pee. They'd all said their good nights, and Benedict had walked off down the street, into the darkness.

She gave herself a little shake, bringing herself back to the present.

'Sorry, what were you saying?'

'CHARITY.' Iris nodded at the piles of Clara's clothes on the floor of her cottage. 'THIS LOT.'

'Did you say Leah had looked through them?'

'WEREN'T YOU LISTENING? YES, SHE DOESN'T WANT ANYTHING.'

Liz looked at the clothes. They were all good quality, and clean. 'Have you gone through the pockets?'

'LEAH DID, LAST NIGHT.'

'Okay.' Liz switched into practical mode. 'Let's bag them up again and I'll take them to Cancer Research.' Liz always donated to Cancer Research rather than any of the other charity shops in the town. It meant going a little out of her way, but if it could make even the slightest difference to the fight against that terrible disease, she thought it was worth it.

They picked up the clothes together, and put them into two bin bags. As Liz was folding a lilac cardigan into one of the bags, something dropped out of it.

'I thought you said Leah had gone through the pockets?'

It was a business card:

Gypsy Rose Young, True Born Romany.
Fortunes told. Advice given.
Health, Romance, Work, Family.
West Pier, Whitby.

Liz showed it to Iris, who nodded.

'SHE WENT THERE, THE MORNING BEFORE SHE...' Iris couldn't bring herself to finish her sentence.

'Why?'

Iris shrugged. 'SHE BELIEVED IN THAT SORT OF STUFF. GOD KNOWS WHY.'

Liz pocketed the card. When they'd done, she shouldered both the bulging bags.

'Right. I'll see you later.'

'DON'T BOTHER COMING BACK TODAY. LEAH'S TAKING ME OUT.'

'That's nice.' Liz was pleased the old lady had something to distract her. 'Where are you going?'

'ON A STEAM TRAIN. TO PICKERING.'

Liz had always promised herself she'd take a trip on the Whitby Heritage Railway, but she still hadn't got round to it. 'Have a lovely time.'

'WE WILL.'

WHEN LIZ GOT BACK to Gull Cottage, she dumped the bags on the kitchen floor, and told herself she'd take them to the charity shop later that afternoon. She had a busy morning ahead of her, as it was changeover day for Kipper Cottage. Helen and Andrew had already left, with promises to come again. Liz hoped they would – they'd been the perfect guests.

Liz got her cleaning caddy from the cupboard under the stairs. Nelson whined.

'You can't come with me. I'll take you out again when I get back, I promise.'

It didn't take her long to do the changeover. Helen and Andrew had tidied the cottage before they left, and, apart from a few stray bulldog hairs, had left everything clean. Liz bundled the dirty towels and sheets into her laundry bag, then made up the bed with clean linen. She cleaned out the grate in the sitting room and re-laid the fire, ready for lighting, restocked the tea caddy with teabags, and the fridge with a bottle of bubbly for her new guests, who would be arriving that afternoon. Finally, she carried out the special request her new guest – Peter – had made over the phone. She took out a bag of faux rose petals from her caddy and tipped them onto the duvet, then shaped them into a heart. It was a Valentine's surprise for Peter's wife Deidre. Although, strictly speaking, it wasn't Valentine's Day until tomorrow, they were coming to Whitby for a romantic getaway.

After double-checking everything was ship-shape and sweet-smelling, Liz lugged her laundry bag and cleaning caddy back to Gull Cottage.

She sensed there was something wrong as soon as she unlocked the door. She had to push the door to get it open, because there was something lying behind it. One of Clara's jumpers. To Liz's dismay, she saw that Nelson had ripped one of the bin bags apart, and its contents were strewn all over the kitchen. She was astonished, and disappointed.

'What on earth's got into you? Bad dog!'

Nelson slunk to his basket. She gathered all the clothes together and pushed them into a corner. She really didn't have time to look for another bag right then.

After taking Nelson for a quick run on Tate Hill Beach, she had to leave him again to take the laundry to the West Cliff. She always used the launderette on the esplanade. Her own washing machine was too old and too temperamental to trust with the letting linen.

She wagged her finger at Nelson as she left. 'Behave yourself this time.'

He gave her an apologetic look, and wagged his tail. It was impossible to stay angry with him for long.

RATHER THAN TAKE the car to the West Cliff, she decided to walk – the laundry bag wasn't too heavy, and the sun was actually shining, which was something of a rarity in February. She had to stop at the swing bridge barrier to wait for a yacht to sail through to the marina, and so took the opportunity to take a few deep breaths of salty air. She knew she was running on automatic, pushing thoughts of Benedict to the back of her mind. But she also knew she would have to stop and think about what had happened – or almost happened – at some point. Her thoughts were interrupted by the bell that indicated the bridge was down again and the barriers were up. She crossed the harbour and headed for St Ann's Staith, towards the fish market and the amusement arcades.

When she had passed the arcades with their clanging sound effects and flashing lights, the road peeled off to her left, up the hairpin bend of the Khyber Pass to the West Cliff above. Liz hesitated.

The west pier stretched out directly ahead of her, punctuated halfway along by its supposedly haunted lighthouse. Tucked in beside the entrance to the pier was a small children's fairground, with a miniature helter-skelter and a carousel. Just in front of them was a brightly painted kiosk. The door was open, and there was a board propped outside it.

Gypsy Rose Young.
True Romany Born. Fortunes told.
Advice given.

Liz stopped and looked at her watch. It would be a rush to get to the launderette and back before her new guests arrived, but Gypsy Rose Young was clearly open for business. Liz's curiosity got the better of her. She hefted her laundry bag more comfortably in her hand, and approached the kiosk.

As she got closer, she could hear someone moving about inside, on the other side of the beaded curtain that hung at the door. She knocked tentatively on the wooden side of the kiosk. There was no answer, so she stuck her head through the curtain.

A woman had her back to her, putting something in a cupboard. 'You took your time,' she said.

'Sorry,' said Liz. 'Were you expecting someone?'

The woman turned. She was tall and raw-boned, with her hair tucked under a multi-coloured scarf. Her long earrings brushed the shoulders of the fisherman's sweater she wore, and all her fingers were adorned with rings, some silver, some gold. She fixed Liz with a dark, disconcerting stare. There was curiosity there, but no sign of surprise.

'You don't want your fortune read,' she said. It was a statement, not a question. Her accent was pure Yorkshire.

'No,' said Liz. 'I was wondering if I could ask you about something.'

'I've a feeling I can't stop you, so you might as well come in and make yourself comfortable. You can drop your washing there.' She pointed to a spot on the floor just inside the door.

Liz did as she was told, only realising as she sat in the chair that there was nothing on her laundry bag to give away its contents. How had Rose known it was washing?

The kiosk was very small, with just enough floor space for two folding chairs and a narrow bamboo table. Every inch of it was decorated. There were embroidered drapes at the window, and many shelves, packed with knick-knacks: a ceramic palmist's hand, a crystal ball, chunks of quartz and amethyst, and photographs, mostly of toddlers and children. Liz assumed they were Rose's grandchildren. The walls were also hung with photographs, also mainly of family. They jostled for space with a set of ornamental daggers and several crucifixes. In pride of place in the corner glowed an illuminated plastic statue of the Madonna and Child. There was so much to look at, but Liz tried to focus on Rose as she settled on the chair.

'How can I help you?' asked Rose.

'A friend of mine came to see you last week. A lady called Mrs Bendelow.'

'And?'

'And... I was wondering... first of all, if you remember her, and secondly, whether there was anything about her visit that sticks in your mind.'

'I knew Clara.' Liz noted Rose's use of the past tense. Rose picked up a deck of cards and shuffled them. 'What do you mean, anything that sticks in my mind?'

Liz shrugged. 'I don't know. How did she seem? Did she ask you about anything in particular?'

Rose cut the deck, and put a card on the table. It had a figure on it, which had one foot stretched out in front of it, about to step out over a cliff. Liz could just make out the words under the illustration – The Fool. She stared at Rose in dismay.

Rose gave her a shrewd look. 'First of all, my lovely, anything that goes on in here is strictly between me and my clients. Dead or alive. And secondly, you weren't really Clara's friend, were you?'

Liz shook her head. 'We have... had... a mutual friend. She's taken it very hard. For her sake, I want to find whoever murdered Clara.'

Rose nodded sympathetically. 'There's some bad folk about.' Rose looked deep into Liz's eyes. She had a very penetrating gaze, but Liz forced herself not to look away. After a tense moment or two, Rose seemed to come to a decision.

'Clara did have a particular question, about someone who had recently come back into her life. But I think you already know what that question was.'

Liz thought she could guess – did Roger Darnton kill Eddie?

'And what was the answer?' she asked.

'Like I said, my readings are confidential.' She saw Liz's disappointment. 'What I *will* say, is that it probably wasn't the answer you'd expect.'

Liz puzzled over that. She wasn't sure what answer she

expected. That Roger Darnton had killed Eddie Bendelow? Had Rose told Clara he hadn't? Liz frowned. Just because the cards said Darnton wasn't a killer, that didn't mean it was true.

Rose was watching her closely.

'As you're here,' she said, 'is there something *you* would like to ask, just for yourself?'

The question caught Liz off guard. 'No. I don't think so.' But she felt her face go hot. There was a question, one that could be framed by a single name: Benedict. But she wasn't about to blurt that out to a complete stranger.

'You don't need to tell me what it is,' said Rose. 'I'll give you the answer anyway.'

Liz scowled. 'I don't have a question.'

Rose didn't seem bothered. She continued in a conversational tone. 'You know, it's a funny thing. The people who come to me, they all have the same kinds of questions. Should they do this... or that? Will they get married? Have kids? But, generally speaking, they already know what they're going to do.'

'They do?'

'Of course they do. Deep down, they've already made their choices. They're already set on a certain course.'

Liz didn't think that was true in her case. She may have decided she wanted to be with Benedict, but that didn't mean he felt the same way. Sometimes it wasn't only a matter of your own choice, but of other people's, too.

'If people already know what they're going to do, why do you bother telling fortunes?' she asked Rose.

Rose grinned, showing the glint of a gold tooth. '*Dukkering* is a living. I try to answer everyone's questions, even though they ask all the wrong ones.'

'What are the right ones?'

Rose's eyes widened. 'Surely you don't expect me to tell

you that? If I gave all my secrets to every Tom, Dick or Harry who came in here I'd be out of a job!'

Liz laughed.

'You should laugh more often, my lovely. It suits you.'

'Thanks. And thanks for talking to me.'

'Any time.'

Liz reached into her pocket. 'Can I give you anything for—'

Rose cut her off with a wave. 'Not this time. We're just two friends, chatting, aren't we? Next time, maybe, when I do a reading for you.'

Liz knew that wasn't going to happen. She saw the laughter in Rose's eyes and realised that Rose knew it, too. They both grinned at each other.

'Thank you,' said Liz.

Rose watched Liz as she headed out through the beaded curtain, then called after her. 'I'll be seeing you.'

LIZ JUST MADE it to the laundry and back to Kipper Cottage before her new guests, Peter and Deidre, arrived from Merseyside. She let them in and told them where everything was. As Deidre was investigating the inglenook fireplace, and admiring the antique poker, Peter took Liz to one side.

'Did you do that thing I asked for, upstairs?' he whispered.

Liz nodded. 'I'll leave you in peace. Don't forget I'm just next door if you need me.'

She went back to Gull Cottage with a smile on her face. Romance was a lovely thing. Her warm fuzzy feeling didn't last long, however, because she started to think, inevitably, about Mark, and then about Valentine's Day... and then, about her missing ruby earring. It still hadn't turned up, and she was beginning to think she must have lost it somewhere while she was out and about. Perhaps it was a sign? A sign that Mark wasn't happy about her potentially budding romance with Benedict? Liz dismissed the thought. She didn't believe in signs, and she certainly didn't believe in life after death.

12

'We'll close the session with a prayer, to protect those who have chosen to make contact with us tonight,' said Hilda Blakey. 'Can you do the honours, please, Graham?'

Graham cleared his throat. 'Blessed are you, O God, for you have created the wide and wonderful world in which we live. We praise you for your constant care for those who have trusted you in ages past, who have crossed into the shady vale. We trust that now you will hold these souls securely in your hands as they follow your call to your side. Through Jesus Christ our Lord. Amen.'

'Amen,' chorused everyone around the table. There was a larger gathering than there had been at the previous session of the Third Eye Society. Roger and the middle-aged couple were there again, but there was no sign of the young girl who had fainted. During the session Hilda had 'made contact' with a number of souls, some of whom had apparently been recognised by people there. The evening was declared a huge success, and everyone chatted animatedly as the session broke up. They all headed to the hall to put on their coats. Hilda took Liz to one side.

'I'm so sorry we haven't made contact with your husband yet, Mrs McLuckie.' Her face was drawn into lines of concern. 'It may be that he has already passed into the light. But we will keep trying.'

Liz just nodded. Her eyes slid to Graham, who was accepting cash from some of the other attendees. Hilda followed her gaze.

'People are so generous,' she said. 'We don't charge for our services, but some people like to show their appreciation. It's very welcome. Graham and I are both retired, you know. It helps make our pensions stretch.'

Liz didn't take the hint. She put on her coat and went out into the night. She'd already decided this would be her last visit to the Third Eye Society. She was getting precisely nowhere as far as Roger Darnton was concerned, and she didn't think she could stomach any more of their performances. The session that night had featured many dead relatives, none of them specific – people whose name began with a T or an S, someone who'd died of a heart attack, a miner, a shopkeeper – each one guaranteed to resonate with somebody in a room full of Yorkshire people. The 'messages' they had passed on were nothing more than platitudes and generalisations.

Liz saw that Roger and the middle-aged couple were standing together half way down the garden path.

'... we'd be so grateful,' said the man to Roger.

Roger patted him on the back. 'I should warn you, though, that I do charge for my services.'

'Whatever it takes,' said the man.

'Thank you.' The woman's voice caught on a sob. 'I just want to know our son Michael is safe and happy.'

Anger seared through Liz. She had to struggle to keep her

eyes averted as she stepped off the path and passed round them. She could feel Roger's gaze burning into her back. She didn't need to be psychic to feel the malevolence that came off the man.

She stomped home in a fury. Roger Darnton was up to his old tricks again. How could anyone take advantage of grieving people like that? Liz knew from hard experience how vulnerable grief could make you. It had been difficult enough for her to lose a husband, but what must it be like to lose a son? No parent should ever have to bury their child. And no one – absolutely no one – should be allowed to take advantage of them.

'What's up with you?' Niall looked up from the pot he was stirring as she came into the kitchen. Leah was setting the table.

'Nothing.' Liz took off her coat. She didn't feel like talking about her evening. Niall picked up on her mood and changed the subject.

'I've asked Leah to stay for dinner, if that's okay?'

'Of course. You're always welcome.' She smiled at Leah, and patted Nelson, who had ambled over to greet her. She realised that Clara's clothes were still piled in a heap in the corner of the room, and made a mental note to put them in a new bin bag and take them to the charity shop the next day. She also spotted Niall's cape hanging on the back of the door.

'Are you doing a ghost tour tonight?' she asked.

Niall nodded. 'A late one. Leah's coming with me.'

'Wild horses couldn't keep me away,' said Leah. 'I'm looking forward to seeing you in action.' She winked at him. Liz pretended not to see.

They had a very pleasant dinner, with Leah telling them about the trip she and Iris had taken on the Heritage railway, and Niall regaling them with tales of his Uncle Fergal, who had worked on the buses in Dublin. He told them about someone trying to transport a donkey, and a neighbour who, with Fergal's help, had managed to move house on the bus, one piece of furniture at a time. As funny as Niall's stories were, Liz only listened with half an ear. She had something more important on her mind.

What on earth was she going to do about Roger Darnton?

BY THE TIME she woke the next morning, she had formulated a plan. She had thought about telling Kevin that Darnton was up to his old tricks, but quickly dismissed the idea. Just because Darnton was taking money off bereaved people, didn't mean he was doing anything illegal this time. The police weren't likely to do anything to stop him.

But she knew someone who might.

She was chomping on a slice of toast when she heard the postie push her mail through the door. One was a bill, which Liz put on the table to open later (then ignore). The other was a plain envelope made from creamy textured paper, addressed to her in capital letters. She opened it.

It was a card. It had a decorative garland embossed on the front, with a small red heart in the centre. Inside, it read...

From an ardent admirer
X

She blinked. She had completely forgotten it was Valentine's Day, and certainly hadn't expected to receive anything. Her first thought was that Niall might be the sender – she knew he'd sent a card to his mum in Dublin, because she'd helped him choose it online. But this wasn't an online card... and the word 'ardent' made her wonder. It was quite a formal, old-fashioned word, not one she imagined Niall would use. She put the card on the mantelpiece, and stared at it. Had Benedict sent it? Or was that just wishful thinking?

She gave herself a shake. How old was she? And what was she doing anyway, mooning around like a love-struck teenager? There was something more important she had to do.

HILDA LOOKED surprised when she answered Liz's knock.

'Mrs McLuckie,' she said.

'Can I come in for a minute?'

Hilda showed her into the dining room where they held their séances. It looked quite different in the daylight, with the sun streaming in and the remains of Hilda and Graham's breakfast on the table.

'Would you like a cup of tea?' offered Hilda. 'There's still some in the pot.'

'No, thanks.'

'Are you okay, Hilda, love?' called a voice. 'Who was that at the door?' Graham appeared in the doorway, wearing a floral apron, with a plate and a tea towel in his hand.

'Is everything okay?' he asked, looking from Hilda to Liz.

Liz lifted her chin. 'I just wanted to tell you something I thought you should know.' She took a breath. 'Roger Darnton is stealing your clients.'

There was a shocked pause.

'He's what?' asked Graham. He put the plate down.

'Stealing your clients. I heard him talking to that couple who was here last night. I don't know their names. They were at both the meetings I came to.'

'Mr and Mrs Becker?' said Graham.

Liz had no idea. It wasn't really important. 'He was saying he'd help them get in touch with their son. Their *dead* son, Michael. For money.'

'The swine!' said Hilda, vehemently.

Liz ploughed on. 'And there's something else you should know. Roger Darnton's an ex-convict. He's been in prison for fraud and blackmail.'

This time, there was no surprise on their faces.

'You already knew?' she asked.

Graham nodded. 'Hilda recognised him when he first got in contact with her. He was quite famous in spiritual circles, you know.'

'He promised not to muscle in on my operation. He *swore* he'd behave himself. I suppose I should have known better.' She glared at Liz. 'You're sure about this?'

'Very sure. I heard it with my own ears.'

'Right!' Hilda got to her feet.

Graham looked alarmed. 'Don't do anything hasty, love.'

'Hasty my arse,' snapped Hilda. 'I should never have let him join. I might have known he'd try to muscle me out. Get my coat!'

Graham scratched nervously at his beard. 'Seriously, love, I think you should take a deep breath, and think about how best to play this. He's not a man you want to cross. We shouldn't just go charging in there.'

Hilda put her hands on her hips. 'Are you going to get my coat, or do I have to get it myself?'

Graham disappeared into the hallway, clearly knowing when he was beaten.

Liz followed them both out of the house. She knew she should probably just leave them to it, and let matters take their course, but, as always, her curiosity got the better of her. She decided to tag along.

Hilda marched ahead, towards the esplanade and the Anchorage Retirement Home.

'I hope you're ready for fireworks,' muttered Graham.

'Once she has a bee in her bonnet, she's like a dog with a bone.'

Mixed metaphors aside, Liz could see he had a point. Every line of Hilda's marching body said she was ready for battle. It seemed Liz had really set something in motion. She'd be lying if she said she regretted it, but she was still a bit concerned about the outcome.

Graham sighed. 'She's always like this. She's a fire sign, you know.'

'How long have you been married?' asked Liz.

'We're not.'

That surprised Liz. She'd thought they were God-fearing Christians.

Graham continued. 'But we've been together for years.'

Liz noticed for the first time that he had a faint Yorkshire accent. 'I take it you're both from Whitby?'

'What makes you think that?'

It seemed an odd response to a perfectly straightforward question. Before Liz could reply, however, she saw they'd reached the Anchorage. The outer door was open, and Hilda marched inside without knocking.

'Here we go,' muttered Graham. 'Strap yourself in.'

Violet Baxter was in the foyer, arranging flowers. 'Hello,' she said. 'How can I help you?'

'I want to speak to Roger Darnton,' snapped Hilda. 'Is he in?'

'I don't know.' Violet wiped her hands on her overall. 'Is he expecting you?'

'That depends whether his third eye is open today.'

Violet was understandably baffled. She looked at Graham for an explanation. He was still wearing his apron and had the tea towel slung over his shoulder, and just looked embarrassed. Violet's eyes moved to Liz. Liz gave an apologetic shrug.

'Well,' snapped Hilda. 'Is he in or isn't he?'

Violet frowned. 'If you hold on a moment, I'll go and see.'

She headed up the stairs. Hilda hesitated, and then set off after her. Not knowing what else to do, Graham and Liz followed.

Violet realised they were all behind her as she was halfway along the upstairs landing. She stopped and turned to face them.

'I really don't think—'

'Don't worry,' soothed Hilda, 'we're old friends. Roger won't mind.'

'She doesn't want the bugger to do a runner,' muttered Graham to Liz, under his breath.

'What room is he in?' demanded Hilda.

'Room nine,' said Violet weakly. Liz felt sorry for her. Hilda was an unstoppable force.

'Lead on, then.'

Room nine was the last one at the end of the corridor. Violet knocked at the door.

'Mr Darnton,' she called, 'you have visitors.'

There was no answer, and no sound of movement inside.

'Try again,' urged Hilda.

Violet knocked again, slightly louder this time. 'Mr Darnton, are you in?'

No answer.

'He must have gone out,' said Violet.

'Rubbish.' Hilda sniffed. 'He's just pretending he's not in, hoping we'll go away.' She tried the door handle. It was unlocked. 'Roger! I have a bone to pick with you.' She pushed the door open and marched inside. Everyone else followed.

The room was gloomy, curtains drawn. For the first few seconds, Liz couldn't see anything amiss. It was a tidy, masculine room. But then she spotted that the bedside lamp had been knocked over. It lay on the rug, in a pool of dark liquid.

There was a long knife beside it, its blade crusted with dried blood.

Roger Darnton was on the bed, arms outflung, mouth open.

Very dead indeed.

Violet screamed.

13

'I've never heard a bigger load of bollocks in my life.' Detective Inspector Fiona Flint glared at Liz over the rim of her plastic cup.

'It's the truth,' protested Liz. 'Clara thought Darnton had murdered her brother, Eddie.'

'The one who killed himself in 1989?' Flint drained her coffee.

'Exactly.'

'So why didn't you tell us this when Mrs Bendelow was murdered?'

'I didn't know about it then. I only found out later, from Iris Gladwell.'

'The same Iris who helped Mrs Bendelow engineer that nonsense with the Ouija board?'

'Yes.'

'So when did you find out that Darnton was an ex-con?'

'About four days after Clara was murdered.'

'Why didn't you come to us then?'

Liz hesitated. She had told Kevin, but she didn't want Flint to know that.

Flint had no intention of letting her off the hook. 'Didn't you think the information might be useful?'

'I did, but...' Liz tailed off helplessly.

Flint stared at her, and her eyes widened. She turned to PC Williams, who had been listening to the interview, his mouth opening and closing in astonishment.

'Williams. Go and get Detective Ossett, will you?'

Williams hurried off to do her bidding. Liz and Flint sat in awkward silence, until he returned a couple of minutes later with Kevin in tow.

'You want me, ma'am?'

'Mrs McLuckie tells me that our latest victim was actually an ex-con, convicted for fraud. Astonishing, isn't it?'

Kevin tried his best, but wasn't able to look suitably astonished.

Flint scowled. 'Why didn't you tell me?'

'I didn't want to bother you with it until I'd checked it out.'

Liz watched Flint struggle with Kevin's answer. It was very plausible.

'And have you?' asked Flint at last. 'Checked it out?'

'Yes, ma'am. I believe it's true.'

Flint's pallor was the only thing that betrayed the fact that she was livid.

'In future,' she said in a measured tone, 'I would be grateful if you could share any information with me as soon as you it.'

'Of course, ma'am. Sorry, ma'am.'

'Now sling your hook.'

'Sorry?'

'Get back to whatever it was you were doing. Mrs McLuckie and I haven't finished our chat.'

Kevin shot Liz a concerned look as he went out.

'For heaven's sake, sit down, Williams,' barked Flint. 'You're giving me a headache.'

Williams sat. Flint turned her attention back to Liz.

'Please remind me, Mrs McLuckie, how many times I've asked you not to get involved in police investigations.'

'It's hardly my fault if—'

Flint held up a hand. 'Cut the crap. You and I both know that none of this happens to you by accident. You insist on poking your nose into other people's business. Business that really has nothing to do with you.'

Liz fell silent. There was some truth in that.

Flint smiled, knowing she'd hit her target. 'I'm not going to tell you again. I wouldn't waste my breath. Instead, I'm going to give you a warning.' She leaned forward. 'If I hear your name again in connection with the murder of Clara Bendelow or Roger Darnton, I *will* arrest you. I *will* charge you with obstructing the course of justice.'

Liz opened her mouth to speak, but Flint cut her off again.

'I know you've heard me say that before. But this time, I promise I *will* do it. I am *itching* to do it.'

Liz blinked at her in dismay.

'Okay.' Flint leaned back in her chair. 'That's all. You can go.'

'WELL?' Tilly looked up from the milkshake she was preparing. 'What happened?'

Liz blew out her lips. 'I got a severe telling-off, that's what happened.'

'He's really dead, then?' asked Mags. 'Mr Darnton?'

'Very, very dead.'

Tilly delivered the coffee and milkshake to her only

customer, a lady with a little girl, then returned to the counter, where Liz had propped herself on a stool.

'Come on, then,' she demanded, 'give us all the gory details.'

'Maybe later,' said Liz. 'I need a cuppa first.'

'Tease,' muttered Tilly.

Mags hurried to fill a teapot from the boiler. 'We should tell Liz *our* good news.'

Liz brightened. 'I could do with some good news.'

'Tilly's come into an inheritance,' said Mags.

'Five thousand pounds,' said Tilly gleefully, 'from someone I didn't even know. A lady called Elizabeth Barker.'

Barker. That rang a bell with Liz. Could it be Bessie Barker, lover of all things pink? Like Liz, Bessie was another shortened form of Elizabeth. 'She didn't live up at the Anchorage, did she?'

'I think she did. But I didn't know her. She was a great aunt, twice removed, or something like that. I'm not sure exactly. I'm not close to my family.' Tilly had been disowned by her parents while she was still in her teens. 'I knew nothing about it until I got a call from her executor, Patricia Haddington.'

It really was a small world. Although, perhaps that wasn't too much of a co-incidence, seeing as Bessie and Patricia had both lived at the Anchorage and Patricia used to be a solicitor.

'Five grand.' Liz whistled. 'I imagine that'll come in handy?'

'Too bloody right it will,' crowed Tilly. 'We can get a new coffee machine. Ours has been on the blink for months.'

'And there'll be plenty left over for a bit of fun,' said Mags with a grin.

'I'll drink to fun.' Liz lifted her tea in a salute. She noticed her hand was trembling, ever so slightly, and lowered it again.

Finding Roger Darnton with his throat cut had affected her more than she cared to admit, even to herself.

'Maybe we should drink to it with something a little bit stronger?' suggested Mags.

Just then, a whirlwind hit the café

'IS IT TRUE?' Iris crashed in through the door, with Leah hot on her heels. 'IS THE BUGGER DEAD?'

The lady customer and her little girl looked up in alarm.

Mags steered Iris to the counter, further away from them.

'I JUST HEARD FROM MIKE HOWSON IN THE FISH SHOP. IS IT TRUE?'

'It is,' said Liz.

'Liz found him,' said Tilly.

'DID YOU?' Iris chuckled and clapped her hands. 'HE GOT WHAT WAS COMING, RIGHT ENOUGH.'

'I'm not sure that's a particularly sensitive thing to say,' admonished Mags, 'when he was murdered.'

'NOT BEFORE TIME, IF YOU ASK ME. IF YOU LIVE BY THE SWORD, YOU DIE BY THE SWORD! IT SAYS SO IN THE BIBLE, DOESN'T IT?'

Liz wasn't sure that the bible was the precise source, but Iris's words struck a chord. Roger Darnton hadn't been killed with a sword, but a knife. She could still picture it in her mind's eye, the curved blade black with dried blood. It was a very unusual knife, and yet...

Her macabre train of thought was derailed by a slap on the back that made her choke on her tea.

'WELL DONE!' Iris beamed at her.

'I only found him,' spluttered Liz. 'I didn't kill him.'

'MORE'S THE PITY. I'D SHAKE YOUR HAND IF YOU HAD.'

The bell on the door jangled as Niall came in. He unclipped Nelson, who scurried behind the counter to find his rubber pig.

'Are you okay?' he asked Liz, anxiously. 'I got in from work, and Nelson had peed on the floor. Then I got a call from Kevin, who said you'd just left the police station.'

'I'm fine,' said Liz. But she suffered a pang of guilt. She should have gone straight home to take Nelson out, rather than come to the café. But she'd been badly in need of human company.

'What happened?' prompted Niall. 'Kevin didn't say much on the phone.'

Liz was about to start her story, when Tilly interrupted.

'Hang on a minute.' She nodded towards the woman and her little girl, who were putting on their coats. She held the door open for them as they went out. When they'd gone, she turned the sign on the door from OPEN to CLOSED.

'It's only half an hour ahead of time,' she said. 'Let's have some privacy.'

When everyone was seated around one of the bigger tables, Liz gave them all an edited version of events, including her overhearing Roger's offer to the middle-aged couple, her decision to tell Hilda, and the dressing-down she'd had from Flint. She left out some of the gorier details of the crime scene, but they were still able to get the gist of it.

Niall whistled. 'Not a great way to go.'

Leah shuddered. Niall squeezed her hand.

'NO MORE THAN THE BUGGER DESERVED.'

Mags smiled. 'Well, I think a celebration is in order.' She nodded at Tilly, who stood up.

'Bubbly, anyone?'

'I won't say no,' said Niall, 'even if it does seem a bit OTT to be celebrating somebody's murder.'

'We're not celebrating *that*,' said Mags, 'we're celebrating Tilly's windfall.'

'Windfall?' echoed Niall.

'An inheritance,' explained Tilly. She produced a bottle of

prosecco from under the counter like a magician pulling a rabbit from a hat.

'A nice one?' asked Niall.

'Nice enough,' said Tilly.

'BETTER THAN A POKE IN THE EYE, I SHOULD THINK,' said Iris. She eyed the bottle dubiously. 'NONE OF THAT FIZZY STUFF FOR ME. DON'T YOU HAVE ANY GIN?'

There was a bit of a scramble as Tilly tried to find a bottle of gin, and everyone else looked for a suitable glass to drink from.

Niall took advantage of the furore to lean in towards Liz.

'You're a dark horse,' he said.

'Eh?'

'Your Valentine's card. I saw it on the mantelpiece.'

'Oh, that.' Liz had completely forgotten about it. Remembering it now gave her a frisson of pleasure.

'Who's it from?' asked Niall.

'I have no idea. That's the whole point of a Valentine's card, isn't it? It's anonymous.'

'Yes, but you must have some idea?'

'None whatsoever.' Liz did her best to look convincing.

'I hope it isn't that bloody Charlie Johnson. Can they send cards from prison?'

His suggestion took the wind out of Liz's sails. Johnson was an unwanted suitor she'd had trouble trying to shake off the year before. Luckily the police had given her a hand, and now he was currently spending time at his Majesty's pleasure for fraud. She really, REALLY hoped the card wasn't from him.

'What are you two whispering about?' asked Mags, as she gave them both a glass of prosecco.

'Liz got a Valentine card this morning,' said Niall.

Liz kicked him under the table.

'Ow!'

'A Valentine, eh?' Tilly winked at Liz.

'WHO'S GOT A VALENTINE?' demanded Iris.

'Liz,' said Niall, moving his leg to avoid another kick. 'We're trying to work out who it's from.'

SQUEAK! Nelson pressed his rubber pig into Liz's lap.

Iris jumped. 'RUDDY DOG! NEARLY GAVE ME ANOTHER HEART ATTACK.' Iris had had a 'cardiac event' the autumn before, but had recovered quickly.

Liz had a little tug of war with Nelson and his pig, grateful that everyone's attention had been deflected from her love life.

Mags raised her glass in a toast. 'To unexpected inheritances.'

'AND DEAD MURDERERS,' added Iris.

Liz raised her glass and took a sip of prosecco. It was ice cold and very delicious. But... she couldn't shake of her feeling of unease. It wasn't just the shock of actually seeing Roger Darnton with his throat cut, but also the questions raised by his death.

If Roger had killed Clara and Eddie, then who had killed Roger? And why?

14

The next morning, Liz took delivery of the new tiles for Gull's bathroom. The delivery driver was in a high bad humour at having to reverse all the way down Henrietta Street because there was nowhere to turn round. It was a cul-de-sac that ended abruptly in the sea, thanks to a landslide a few years before that had swept away the cottages at the end of the terrace. Liz knew was only a matter of time before Kipper and Gull went the same way, but it didn't worry her too much. She'd be long gone by then.

She eyed the huge flat-bed truck with the mechanical arm that was idling in front of her door. It was blocking the street entirely.

'I did tell your office they would have to make the delivery with a van rather than a truck,' she said to the unimpressed driver.

'Aye, well, they didn't tell me that, did they?' He thrust the paperwork at Liz to sign. 'Where do you want the pallet?'

'Pallet?'

'The wooden pallet your goods are on.'

'Oh. I don't really want a pallet as well.'

The driver shrugged. 'That's the way they come.' He asked her to stand back and then remotely controlled the crane to lower the pallet of tiles in front of Liz's doorstep. Then he simply drove off, leaving her high and dry with a huge pallet almost blocking her doorway.

Liz sighed. Niall was at work, so she had no choice but to start moving the tiles herself.

It took ages. Once she'd freed the tiles from the plastic strapping them to the pallet, she had to take them upstairs to the bathroom, one box at a time. It only took her a couple of trips to regret she'd decided to tile the walls completely, rather than just halfway up. By the time the bathroom was stacked with boxes, there was barely room to get to the toilet and shower, but she supposed it was better than having them piled in the living room or kitchen. It would be inconvenient until the tiler arrived, but she and Niall were used to inconvenience.

She'd just taken the last box up, when she heard someone call out from downstairs.

'Hello? Liz?'

Yip, yip, yip!

She dumped the box and staggered back down stairs.

To her surprise, it was Irwin, Iris's son, peering over the pallet through the open door into the kitchen. Nelson wagged his tail at him.

'You'll have to climb over that, Irwin, if you want to come in. Sorry.'

He picked his way over the wood, being careful not to mark his shiny brogues. He was immaculate, as always, in a shirt and tie and Fair Isle jumper.

'When did you get back?' asked Liz. She dropped into a chair, her legs weak from her exertions.

'Last night,' he said.

'Was it a good conference?'

'Very good, thank you. There were some excellent lectures on green burials.' Irwin worked at the local undertakers in Sandsend. He was in his fifties and, having never married, lived on his own in a tiny but stylish flat on the West Cliff. He sat down opposite her at the table.

Liz got her breath back, and remembered her manners.

'Can I get you a cup of tea?'

'No, thank you. I've just been to Mum's. She almost drowned me in it.' He looked her over. 'I hear you've been having some drama.'

Liz raised her eyebrows. 'You could say that.'

'Why didn't you call me?'

'I didn't want you to come rushing back from your conference. It wasn't anything we couldn't handle.'

Irwin's forehead was wrinkled with concern. 'Mum's cottage is in a terrible state.' His gaze slid around Liz's kitchen, which was hardly any better, with its units ripped out and Clara's clothes still piled in the corner.

Liz felt a flash of embarrassment.

'And it isn't just the mess,' he continued. 'When I was there this morning she accidentally put the milk in her washing machine. She was absent-minded enough before I went away, but now... I think she's worse.'

Liz tried to reassure him. 'It might just be temporary. Clara's death has really shaken her up.'

'She says you went with her to look at the room at the Anchorage?'

'I did, but it was too pink. I told her she could paint it, but she wasn't interested.'

'Just like mother. Stubborn as a mule. I suggested she might take another look at it, but she said, "I'M OKAY WHERE I AM, THANK YOU VERY MUCH, NOW I HAVE LEAH TO LOOK AFTER ME."'

His impression of Iris was quite good, with the volume

and intonation exactly right. He and Liz grinned at each other.

'Leah seems nice,' he said, 'but she's not going to be around forever, is she?'

'No.' They both knew that she was hardly a long-term solution.

'I need go to the Anchorage and have a chat with Mrs Baxter,' he said. 'See what the situation is. It'll have to wait until the weekend, though. I have to go into work this afternoon.'

'I can go, if you like?' Liz was quick to volunteer. She was quite keen to see what was happening at the Anchorage in the wake of the police investigation. As long as she didn't bump into Detective Inspector Flint.

Irwin hesitated. 'If you're sure you don't mind? I don't want to put you to any more trouble.'

'I don't mind at all. Honestly.' The thought occurred to her that there would now be three rooms free, and potentially a shortage of takers, under the circumstances of their evacuation. She thought Violet Baxter might be pleased to see her.

'WHAT DO YOU WANT?'

It was hardly the welcome Liz expected. It threw her off her stride.

'Um... I can come back another time if it's more convenient?' A staff member had shown her into the small, windowless room that served as Violet's office. It was furnished with a couple of old filing cabinets and a desk piled high with paperwork.

Violet Baxter sighed and rubbed her eyes. 'I'm sorry, Mrs McLuckie. Things have been a little tense here.' That had to be the understatement of the century, with two murders committed on the premises in less than a fortnight. 'Come in, have a seat.'

Liz cleared some papers off the chair to sit down.

'I never did ask,' said Violet, 'what it was that Mrs Blakey was so angry with Mr Darnton about?'

'Just a professional disagreement.'

'You don't think she...?'

Liz shook her head. 'She was as shocked as I was... She's taken it hard. I've heard she won't get out of bed.' That snippet of information had come from Mike Howson.

'So how can I help you?' asked Violet.

'I was wondering what the situation might be with your spare rooms? Mrs Gladwell's son is still very keen for her to come here.'

'What was the problem with Bessie Barker's room, again?'

'Too pink.'

'Ah. Yes, Bessie did like pink. Pink and purple.'

'I suppose we should be grateful she decorated with the former rather than the latter.'

Violet just looked puzzled. Liz realised her sense of humour had missed the mark.

'Mrs Bendelow's room is free,' said Violet, 'but Mr Darnton's... there's someone coming to clean it up this afternoon. I'll certainly give Mrs Gladwell first refusal.' She said that with the air of someone bestowing a huge favour. Liz was amused. She could hardly imagine there'd be people queuing round the block to take the murder rooms.

'I'll also get our handyman to give the pink room a coat of paint. Mrs Gladwell can take another look at that, too, if she likes.'

'That would be fantastic.' Liz got to her feet. 'I'll tell Irwin he can bring her along later in the week.'

'Please do.'

'I can see you're busy,' said Liz. 'I'll see myself out.'

As she passed the open drawing room door, she could see Dickie Ledgard and Max Plum playing chess. Dickie raised his hand as he spotted her. She waved back. She felt very sorry for him and the other residents. It couldn't be easy living in the middle of so much horror and disruption.

She was approaching the front door when Patricia Haddington pushed her way in, laden with shopping bags, huffing and puffing as she heaved them into the hallway. Liz hurried to hold the door open for her.

'Can you manage? Would you like a hand upstairs?'

'That would be marvellous, thank you.'

Liz took two of the bags and followed Patricia up the stairs. But as they reached the top of the stairs, and turned down the corridor, Liz felt suddenly nauseous. The closer they got to the room at the end of the corridor, the worse she felt. She could feel the blood draining from her face. Her heart started to pound.

'This is me,' said Patricia as they arrived at room eight. She turned and saw the look on Liz's face.

'Good Lord! Are you ill?'

'Not... not really,' gasped Liz. 'It's just being here, next to Roger Darnton's room ... brings it all back.'

'Ah, of course,' Patricia peered at Liz. 'You found poor old Roger, didn't you? Don't you fret; I have just the thing to put you right.'

She ushered Liz into her room. It was very tidy, with a narrow single bed and one rather uncomfortable-looking armchair beside the fireplace. There were a dozen or so photographs on the walls, most of them of horses, some with rosettes pinned to the frames. There was something very jolly hockey sticks and girls' boarding school about it. Patricia rummaged in a cupboard, and brought out a small bottle and two glasses.

'I think we can have a restorative nip, don't you, as the

sun's over the yardarm.' She didn't wait for Liz's answer, but poured them both a generous slosh of brandy. Liz spotted a pile of wallpaper samples and colour charts on the desk. Patricia followed her gaze.

'I thought I'd gussie the place up a bit,' she said. 'You can go slightly ga-ga in here, staring at the same walls for months on end.' She gave Liz a glass and clinked hers against it. 'Bottoms up.'

'Cheers.' The brandy burned Liz's throat, but it did make her feel better.

Patricia finished hers in a couple of gulps. She picked up two of the wallpaper samples and held them against the wall.

'What do you think?' she asked. 'I like the floral one, but the stripes are quite nice too.'

Liz considered them. 'The flowers, I think,'

'Do you think so?' Patricia looked at them doubtfully. 'You might be right. I don't really have an eye for these things. Bessie used to keep me straight.'

'Bessie Barker?'

Patricia nodded. 'This old place really isn't the same without her. We'd known each other for years.' She picked up one of the photos from the desk and passed it to Liz. 'This is her in her younger days, when she was a student nurse.'

It was a black and white photo of a woman in an old-fashioned nurse's uniform. Liz's eyes widened. Apart from the dark hair, which she could just see under her starched cap, Bessie Barker looked astonishingly like Tilly.

'Of course, you're Bessie's executor, aren't you?' she said. 'Mathilda Fairweather, a good friend of mine, was one of her beneficiaries.'

'The *only* beneficiary. Bessie left everything else to the Yorkshire Home for Retired Dray Horses. She was scrupulously fair. She knew her great niece Wendy had had a daughter, and felt she should make provision for her.' Patricia eyed Liz speculatively. 'Mathilda's had something of a colourful history.'

Liz admired Patricia's tact. Tilly had, in fact, spent years in foster homes, and then in a Young Offenders Institution, where she'd met Mags. Luckily, it had all turned out well in the end.

'Friendship's a funny thing, isn't it?' mused Patricia. 'Especially old ones. Bessie and I stuck together through thick and thin, even when she was diagnosed with dementia.' She blinked back a tear, and put the photograph back on the desk.

'I hadn't realised you and Mrs Barker were so close.'

'*Miss* Barker. Bessie never married, same as me. Of course, she was as daft as a brush at the end, but I still miss her.' Patricia took a handkerchief from the pocket of her tweed waistcoat to wipe her eyes. 'Look at me,' she sniffed. 'Ridiculous. You think I'd be used to death at my age. It's just part of the scenery in here.'

'It's different when it's someone you love, though, isn't it?'

'Yes.' There was desolation in Patricia's eyes. 'It is.'

Liz wondered. Patricia had been at pains to tell her neither she nor Bessie had ever married. Could they have been more than friends? If so, Bessie's death must have been doubly devastating for her. Triply so, if their relationship had been a secret and she felt she couldn't mourn her properly.

'Still...' Patricia made an effort to pull herself together. 'Life marches on, eh?' She picked up the brandy bottle. 'How about another nip?'

15

Liz coughed.

Even though she was wearing a protective mask and goggles, the dust still clogged her throat and nose. She gave the tiles another whack with her hammer and chisel, and was dismayed when only half a tile fell to the floor. At this rate, it was going to take her all day to get all the tiles off the bathroom wall, and another day to fill and sand the walls before the tiler could put the new ones up. She'd decided to do the prep herself to save money, but was regretting it now. She put her chisel down. Her throat was parched. She needed a cup of tea. She stepped out of the cloud of plaster dust onto the landing, and climbed over the boxes of new tiles to get down the stairs.

Nelson barked at the sight of her. She remembered she was still wearing her mask and goggles, and took them off.

'It's just me, daftie.'

Nelson looked relieved, and settled back into his basket as she went to put the kettle on.

There was a knock at the front door. Kevin recoiled slightly when she answered it.

'I'm tiling,' she said, to explain her dusty appearance. 'Or rather, un-tiling.'

'I thought you'd gone white overnight. They say trauma can do that.' She hadn't seen him to speak to since the day she'd found Roger Darnton. She ushered him in.

'How are you?' he asked

'I'm fine.'

'Really?'

Liz nodded. She didn't want to worry him by telling him she kept having surges of panic, and flashbacks of Roger lying on his bed, like a bloodied puppet with its strings cut. The funny turn she'd had outside Patricia's had just been her first. She'd had two more since, once after she'd got home and another in bed that morning. It had occurred to her she should probably seek counselling, but she wasn't quite sure where to start with that. In the meantime, there was always tea.

'I've just put the kettle on,' she said. 'Do you have time for a cuppa?'

'It'll have to be a quick one. Flint's driving us like galley slaves.'

Liz made tea for them both. They sat at the table to drink it.

'Are there any new developments?' she asked. She couldn't help herself. 'Are the DNA results back yet?'

'Mmm,' Kevin murmured noncommittally into his mug.

'Was that a yes or a no?'

Kevin nodded. 'Yes.'

'And?'

Kevin shrugged. 'Much as we expected.'

Liz narrowed her eyes.

'What's this?' Kevin jumped up and went to the fireplace. 'A Valentine's card?' He took it off the mantelpiece and read it aloud. '*From an ardent admirer.*'

Liz blushed. She hadn't seen Benedict at all since. She was beginning to think he was avoiding her. Again.

Kevin gave her a shrewd look. 'Do you know who it's from?'

'Do you?'

'Not officially. But I do know the handwriting.'

Liz's heart soared. So it *was* from Benedict!

Kevin returned the card thoughtfully to the mantelpiece. Liz knew he was aware of how she felt about his father, although they'd never actually spoken about it.

'How would you feel, Kevin, if me and your dad...' She didn't finish the sentence, but saw his hesitation. 'You can be honest.'

'I just want you both to be happy. Although...'

'Although?'

'I do worry it might spoil our friendship.'

'Would it have to?'

Kevin shrugged. 'It would definitely change it, wouldn't it?'

Liz nodded. 'I suppose it would.' Change was inevitable. It didn't have to be a negative thing... but his reaction made her think. Her relationship with Kevin was something she really valued. If things didn't work out between her and Benedict, would it sour her relationship with Kevin? Was that a risk she was willing to take?

AFTER KEVIN HAD GONE, Liz attacked the bathroom tiles with renewed vigour. It helped to have something physical to do to take her mind off Benedict, Roger and everything else. By the time Niall got in from work, she'd managed to work her way round three quarters of the walls. Niall made them both a mushroom risotto, which she ate in her overalls, and then she went back to finish the job. Afterwards, physically and mentally exhausted, she asked Niall if he could take Nelson out for his last walk of the night, then she swept the tiling debris into bin bags, and went to bed dirty. She had no choice, because the shower was out of action until the walls were tiled again. She fell into a deep, immediate sleep.

BENEDICT KISSED HER, a long, luxurious kiss that took her breath away. Then he laughed, and showed her the knife behind his back.

'Here's Benny!' he cackled as he lunged towards her with the blade.

She ran for it, along the landing at the Anchorage. Doors flashed past her – number four, number two, number seven. The corridor stretched out in front of her – number six, number one, number five. She felt a hand clutch her jacket, and wrenched herself free. Suddenly she was in front of room eight. The number coiled like a snake on the door. She burst into the room and, ignoring the carnage on the bed behind her, slammed the door on Benedict's leering face.

He beat the flimsy wood with his fist. Somehow she could see him doing it, even though she was on the other side. She could hear him too: BANG BANG.

'Let me in, Liz! You know you want to!'

BANG BANG BANG.

Liz jerked out of sleep, her heart hammering.

BANG BANG BANG.

Yip yip yip!

Hearing Nelson bark, she realised the banging wasn't in her dream at all, but that there was someone actually pounding on the door downstairs. She struggled to pull herself together. What a terrible dream! As she clawed her way fully back to consciousness, she heard Niall thump down the stairs, and heard him open the front door.

Then she could hear voices, but couldn't make out whose they were.

Niall called up the stairs.

'LIZ! ARE YOU AWAKE? YOU'D BETTER COME DOWN.'

She looked groggily at her watch. Quarter past three. She dragged herself out of bed, and found her dressing gown and slippers.

She was greeted downstairs by a sight she really didn't expect to see at that time in the morning – Iris and Leah, hair plastered over their faces, shivering and dripping water onto the kitchen floor.

Suddenly she was wide awake.

'What on earth...?' she began

'WE'VE HAD A LITTLE ACCIDENT,' said Iris.

'A leak,' elaborated Leah. 'It came through the ceiling.'

Liz put the heating on. 'Niall, can you get some towels? There's plenty in the airing cupboard.'

Niall hurried upstairs to get them.

'Are you both okay?' asked Liz.

'Just a bit cold and wet,' said Leah.

'WE'RE FINE. IT'S NOTHING THAT CAN'T BE FIXED.' Iris spotted Liz picking up her phone. 'WHAT ARE YOU DOING?'

'Calling Irwin.'

'DON'T BE DAFT. WE DON'T NEED TO BOTHER HIM. JUST GIVE US A BED FOR THE NIGHT AND WE'LL SORT IT OUT IN THE MORNING.'

Liz was too tired to argue.

Niall re-joined them, and gave Iris and Leah a bath towel each. 'Is the water still coming through?' he asked Leah. 'I can go and find the stopcock.'

Leah's teeth chattered as she answered. 'It's okay. It's stopped.'

Liz shifted into practical mode. 'Let's get you both warmed up and into bed.'

She steered Iris upstairs to her bedroom, where she helped her towel herself dry and get into a pair of her pyjamas. Then, once Iris was safely tucked up in bed with a hot water bottle, Liz went back downstairs.

'Feeling any better?' she asked Leah.

'Much better, thanks.' Leah had also dried off and changed into a pair of Niall's tracksuit bottoms and one of his sweaters. She looked very cosy.

'It wasn't a leak, Liz.'

'No?'

Leah shook her head. 'Iris left the taps running in the bathroom sink. With the plug in. I think the whole ceiling's come down.'

'Shit,' said Niall.

Liz couldn't argue with that summary of the situation. It was bad news – not only because the water would have caused so much damage, but because Iris had caused the flood in the first place. Her absent-mindedness was more than just worrying now.

'I'll call Irwin in the morning,' she said, 'and let him know what's going on.' It was a pity Iris hadn't liked Bessie Barker's room. She would be much better off somewhere where somebody could keep an eye on her full time. As long as she wasn't murdered, too. Liz shook off that morbid thought, and turned her attention to more pressing matters. Where was Leah going to sleep?

'I have an inflatable mattress I can put down for you in here?' she suggested. 'Or, if you'd rather, you can bunk in with Iris and I can sleep down here?'

Niall and Leah exchanged a look.

'I think we'll manage,' said Niall, with a grin.

'Oh?' It took Liz a second to get it. She still wasn't firing on all cylinders. 'Oh. Alright then. I'll say goodnight to you both.'

Iris was snoring lustily when Liz crept into bed beside her. As Liz lay in the darkness, she could hear the murmur of voices in Niall's room below. She couldn't help but feel a pang of envy. Young love!

It took ages for her to get warmed up again, but gradually she relaxed, and her eyes drifted closed. Suddenly – horrifyingly – Benedict was in front of her, his knife raised aloft, the blade crusted with dried blood. Liz's eyes flashed open. And stayed open. The knife was the same one she'd seen on Roger Darnton's floor. It was very distinctive, with a long, curved blade and an elaborate hilt. She frowned. There was something nagging at the back of her brain.

She swung her legs out of bed, and found her dressing gown in the darkness. Then she crept down to the sitting room and switched on her laptop. When the ancient machine had groaned into action, Liz went online. She typed 'kinds of dagger' into the search bar.

There were a lot of results. She scrolled through them until she found what she was looking for – a photo of a knife similar to the murder weapon, with a curved blade and carved hilt. She clicked on the link and discovered it was a najava, a type of Andalusian folding knife commonly found in Northern Spain... and in Romany culture.

16

'**G**ood Lord,' muttered Irwin. 'What a mess.'

He prodded a chunk of plaster that had once been part of the ceiling with the toe of his brogue. He and Liz were standing in Iris's bedroom on the second floor of Benbow Cottage. Most of the ceiling lay in sodden pieces around their ankles, and they could see right up, through the bathroom, to the roof beams above.

'You're lucky the bath didn't come down, too,' said Liz.

It was clear from Irwin's expression he didn't feel lucky. Everything was soaked. Iris's patchwork quilt sagged on the iron bedstead, the rugs squelched when you trod on them, and even the curtains were wet through. They hung so heavily on their pole that that one of end of it had pulled away from the wall, and it was leaning crazily over the window.

'How on earth am I going to sort this out?' asked Irwin.

Liz's tone was bracing. 'The same way you eat an elephant.'

'Sorry?'

'One bite at a time. The first thing is to rescue what we can of Iris's things and move her out.'

Irwin nodded. 'She can stay with me. I'll sleep on the floor.'

'Violet Baxter says you can take her to look round the rooms at the Anchorage tomorrow. With any luck, she'll see one she likes.'

'I'm not holding my breath about that.' His bleak gaze slid to Liz. 'Also...'

Liz looked at him. 'Also?'

'I'm supposed to be in York tomorrow. It's not something I can get out of.' He hesitated. 'Or, if I'm honest, it's not something I *want* to get out of. It's an interview.'

'I thought you were happy at Carlyle's?' Irwin had worked at Thomas Carlyle Funeral Directors in Sandsend for a long time. Liz hadn't realised he was looking for a new job.

Irwin shrugged. 'It doesn't hurt to have a look about every now and then. Even if I stay where I am, I might get a pay rise out of it.'

'Okay. Don't worry about Iris. I'll take her.'

'I'm really sorry about all this, Liz. You've done so much already. It's hardly fair.'

'You're my friend, Irwin. So is Iris. If I can help out, I will.'

He hugged her. 'Thank you.' Then his eyes widened. 'What about Leah? She won't have anywhere to stay, either.'

Liz smiled. 'I'm sure Niall won't mind her bunking up with him for a while.'

'Oh,' said Irwin, arching his eyebrow. 'Like that, is it? I hadn't realised.'

'It's new. But they seem quite smitten with each other. And I've no objections to an extra lodger...'

·   ·   ·

When Liz got back to Gull Cottage, she was surprised to see Niall making breakfast for himself, Leah and Iris.

'Why aren't you at work?' she asked.

'I called in sick. Stretched the truth a bit, and said the flood was here. So me and Leah can help out at Benbow.'

'YOU'RE A GOOD LAD,' said Iris. She turned to Liz. 'HE'S A GOOD LAD, ISN'T HE?'

'He is,' agreed Liz. 'You want to be careful, though. You don't want the museum to think you're slacking.'

'I'm not sure I care, to be honest. I'm so bored there.'

'You'd miss the money, though.'

'Ah, that's true, right enough.'

They all spent the morning at Benbow, rescuing what they could of Iris's belongings, while Iris wandered about, picking up things that were ruined, muttering darkly about the short-falls of modern plumbing.

'THIS WOULDN'T HAVE HAPPENED IN THE OLD DAYS, WHEN WE HAD A STANDPIPE IN THE YARD.'

'Don't give me that,' snapped Irwin. 'The flood might not have happened, but diphtheria and dysentery would. And so would tuberculosis and polio.'

Iris sniffed, but didn't argue. Irwin was generally pretty easy going, but when he did take a stand, he was unmovable.

They carried everything they could save to the Full Moon Café, where Tilly had cleared space in her store room. Then Iris settled in at the café for the afternoon, while Irwin headed to work and Niall, Leah and Liz returned to Gull Cottage.

Liz dropped wearily into one of the kitchen chairs. 'There's an errand I need to run, but I should get started on filling and sanding the bathroom walls. The tiler's coming tomorrow.'

'Sure, we can do that,' said Niall. 'Can't we, Leah?'

Leah nodded. 'No problem. Just show us where you keep your tools.'

Grateful for their help, Liz took Nelson with her, to keep him out of their way. She took him down to Tate Hill beach for a quick pee, before heading through the town to the west pier. Even though it was chilly, the sun was shining. It raised Liz's spirits to see the sparkle of sunlight off the sea. Winter in Yorkshire could feel interminable, with a sizable chunk of it seeming to have barely any daylight at all, but on a day like today, with the sun shining and the seagulls squabbling over-head, she could almost believe that spring wasn't too far away.

They turned right when they crossed the bridge, down the pedestrian walkway of St Ann's Staith. When they got past the amusement arcades, Liz could hear raised voices. She saw a group of five or six people at the entrance to the pier, in front of Rose Young's kiosk. They had placards. As she got closer Liz could read what a couple of them said.

Fight the forces of ignorance.

Say no to gypsy superstition.

Nelson growled, low in his throat. Liz looked at him, surprised. He almost never growled, except... Liz searched the figures and found one wearing a tweed coat and old-fash-ioned cloche hat. Nelson pulled her towards the little group, hackles raised.

Dora spotted them. 'Keep that dog away from me!'

'What are you doing?' asked Liz.

'Isn't it obvious? We're saving people from their own igno-rance.' Dora brandished her placard:

Say no to Romany lies.

Liz looked at the kiosk. She could see a dark shape inside – Rose was watching them through the window.

'Have you had this action approved by the Sceptics Society?' Liz demanded. 'I can't imagine you have. You do realise that this protest is racist?'

'Don't be absurd,' said Dora. 'I'm not racist!'

Nelson's growls were now interspersed with frantic whimpers. He was pulling at his lead, desperate to get to Dora's ankles. Liz strained to hold him back.

'Perhaps you should take a proper look at some of your placards,' she suggested to Dora.

'We're not protesting about gypsies, *per se*,' piped up another member of the group, a tall youth with a wispy beard. He kept one concerned eye on Nelson as he addressed Liz. 'We're protesting about what they do. About them taking advantage of the gullible.'

'That's a very fine distinction,' said Liz. She took her mobile phone from her pocket. 'I'm not sure the police would see it that way.'

Dora lifted her chin. 'Go on. Call them. We're taking a stand against hocus pocus! We have a right to protest!'

The other protesters nodded, but Liz could see some looked less than convinced. But Dora had called her bluff. Liz realised another tactic – her final deterrent – was necessary. She bent to unclip Nelson's collar from the lead.

'What are you doing?' squeaked Dora in alarm.

'We have a right to protest, too. Against ignorance and racism. Don't we, Nelson?'

Nelson barked. He could sense that victory – aka Dora's ankles – was almost in reach.

'Don't you dare let that dog of yours loose on me!'

Liz just gave Dora a level stare, her hand on the clip. She

would never actually set Nelson on Dora, of course, but Dora didn't know that. Not for sure.

Dora glared at her, then turned to the others. 'Come on,' she snapped. 'I think we've made our point.'

Liz waited until the muttering little group was out of sight, before knocking at the kiosk door. Rose opened it.

'Are you okay?' asked Liz. 'Does that happen very often?'

Rose shrugged. 'Often enough. I never tangle with them. I could argue till I was blue in the face and they'd never see things my way.' She tapped her forehead. 'They've already made up their tiny little minds.'

Liz smiled. 'Do you have a minute?' she asked. 'I can tie Nelson up out here.'

Nelson gave her a wounded look. She suspected it wasn't so much at the prospect of being tied up, than the fact she'd denied him access to Dora's ankles.

'I don't normally let dogs indoors,' said Rose, 'but I'll make an exception for my hero.' She grinned at Nelson. 'Come in, both of you.'

To Liz's surprise, once they were inside, Nelson sat at Rose's feet, as if he'd known her all his life. As Liz sat in the other chair, her eyes went straight to the display of ornamental knives she'd seen on her last visit. One of them – the largest – was almost identical to the knife that had cut Roger Darnton's throat.

Rose saw her interest. '*Churi najavas*,' she said. 'But I've a feeling you already know that.'

'I don't suppose you have one missing, do you?'

'Why?'

Liz hesitated. 'Did you hear about the man who was murdered last weekend? Up at the Anchorage?'

'Yes. I read about it in the *Bugle*. Bad business.'

'I probably shouldn't tell you this, but he was killed with a knife almost exactly the same as that one.' Liz pointed to the largest najava.

'Really?' Rose looked at it, her expression unreadable. 'Are you sure?'

'Very sure.' Liz nodded. 'I saw it myself. At the scene. '

Rose gave Liz a dark look. 'So why have you come to me?'

'I wanted to see if you had one missing.'

'You think I killed him?'

'No! Not at all. I thought someone might have stolen one.'

'What makes you think I didn't?'

'Pardon?'

'What makes you think I didn't kill him?'

'I don't know.' Liz frowned, wrong-footed. 'You didn't, did you?'

'No.' Rose shook her head, exasperated. 'You're missing my point, lovely.'

Liz just looked at her.

'My point is,' continued Rose, 'that you go marching in with both feet, where anyone with any sense would think twice.'

Liz didn't like to think of herself as having no sense, but she supposed she did have the habit of plunging into situations without thinking. It had got her into trouble before. Serious trouble.

'Point taken,' she said. 'I'll be more careful in future.'

Rose laughed. 'I doubt that.' Her expression grew sombre again. 'Now you can see all my najavas are present and correct, what are you going to do about it? Do the police know what kind of knife it was?'

'Not as far as I know. But I suppose Kevin will be researching it.' Liz saw Rose's puzzled look. 'He's one of the investigating detectives.'

'You don't think the killer is Rom?'

'Not necessarily. Anyone can buy a najava, I suppose. Online?'

'I suppose.' Rose nodded, but her eyes were unfathomable.

It occurred to Liz that it was still quite a coincidence to come across two rare, yet virtually identical, knives within the space of a couple of days. But Rose spoke again, derailing her train of thought.

'I hear you like to solve murders?'

'I do,' said Liz. 'Although it's mostly by accident and luck, rather than design.'

'Who are your suspects for this one?'

Liz thought about it. 'Well, this is actually the second murder at the Anchorage, so the obvious suspects are the residents. And Violet Baxter – although, to be fair, I really don't think she expected to find Roger dead like that. Unless she's an Oscar-worthy actress, I think we can rule her out. That leaves Dickie Ledgard, Max Plum, and Patricia Haddington. Do you know any of them?'

'I know Patricia. Or rather, I knew her mother, Amanda. We were friends. I haven't spoken to Patricia since Amanda's funeral.'

Something in Rose's expression prompted Liz to ask a question.

'Did you fall out with her? With Patricia?'

'Let's just say we had an exchange of words.'

'What about?'

'I don't like to spread gossip, lovely.' Rose bent to scratch Nelson under his chin as he gazed up at her adoringly. 'Let's just leave it at that, shall we?'

17

M ike Howson was more than happy to supply the information Rose Young had withheld. 'She accused her of killing her mother, right there in the church,' he said as he bent to tuck a herring back under the ice in his box.

Liz was puzzled. 'Rose's mother? Murdered in the church?'

Mike rolled his eyes. '*Patricia's* mother. Rose accused her in the church, at the funeral. Everyone knew there was no love lost between them.'

'Between Rose and Patricia?' Liz was struggling to keep up.

'Between Patricia and her mother. They'd been estranged for years.'

'But what made Rose think Patricia murdered her?'

'Amanda Haddington was very ill. Terminal. She summoned Patricia. Then she died suddenly, just hours after Patricia got there. The coroner's verdict was she'd got her pills mixed up by accident.'

'If Amanda Haddington was already dying, why would Patricia murder her?' asked Liz.

Mike shrugged. 'Most folk took that view. They thought Rose was bang out of order. She wasn't popular in the town to begin with.'

'WHAT ARE YOU TWO GOSSIPING ABOUT IN THE MIDDLE OF THE STREET?' They'd been so intent on their conversation that they hadn't heard Iris approach.

'Gossiping? Me?' Mike feigned outrage. 'You know me better than that, Mrs G.' He ignored her withering look. 'You're up and about early. First up gets the shoes, eh?'

An old Whitby saying. In the days when fishing families had many children, they could often only afford a few pairs of shoes to share between them. Whoever got up first, would have shoes to wear that day.

Iris ignored Mike's attempt at banter. 'LIZ IS TAKING ME UP TO THE ANCHORAGE,' she said bleakly. 'IRWIN'S FORCING ME TO LIVE THERE.' She glanced at Liz, as if daring her to contradict her. Liz said nothing.

Mike didn't pick up on the contentious statement either. 'The Anchorage, eh? Well, be sure to give Dickie Ledgard my best.'

'Is he a friend of yours?' asked Liz, glad to have the conversation back on a neutral footing.

'He is. And he's won me quite a bit of cash over the years.' Mike saw Liz's puzzled look. 'He's a jockey. Or used to be. Only just pipped at the post for English champion back in the day. I always bet on him.' Mike glanced at his watch, and pulled a face. 'Got to dash. See you later. See you later, Mrs G.'

Iris just nodded to him, as he headed for the smokehouse next door. She turned to Liz.

'ARE WE OFF, THEN?' she said. 'I HAVEN'T GOT ALL DAY.'

'We'll go in a bit. We just have to wait for the tiler. He shouldn't be long.'

THE TILER WAS LATE, something to do with an accident on the Guisborough Road, which made Iris even grumpier than she was already. By the time she and Liz found themselves standing in front of the Anchorage, Iris's whole body was stiff with the expectation of umbrage-to-come. Liz knew she was going to have her work cut out.

Inside, they found Violet on her knees, tidying out the store cupboard in the dining room. The floor was strewn with lengths of tinsel, old-fashioned glass baubles and a couple of tatty-looking wreaths – legacies, Liz guessed, from residents gone before. The ghosts of Christmases past.

'Good morning, Mrs Gladwell.' Violet got to her feet and dusted herself off. 'I'm so pleased you agreed to come back for another look. We've had the pink room painted a nice neutral colour, and there are also another two rooms free now. I'm sure one of them will suit you.'

Iris sniffed. 'WE'LL SEE ABOUT THAT.'

They looked at Bessie Barker's ex-pink room first.

'IT'S STILL QUITE SMALL,' was Iris's verdict.

Violet glanced at Liz. A coat of paint wasn't likely to have made it any bigger, although Liz thought the new colour – a warm cream – was a definite improvement.

'LET'S SEE ANOTHER ONE.'

They went to Clara's old room. It looked much the same as it had when they cleared out Clara's things.

'I CAN'T SLEEP IN HERE,' said Iris, in a tone that brooked no argument. 'TOO MANY MEMORIES.'

Liz thought that was fair enough. They were down to the last room now – Roger Darnton's. Liz did her best to hide her agitation as they walked down the corridor towards it, but still found her heart beating erratically as they approached the door. She saw Violet's face as she pushed the door open, and realised that she felt much the same way. Inside, there was no sign of Roger Darnton's terrible end, or of the police investigation. The bed had been stripped, and the room was bare apart from a new, large rug. Blood was notoriously difficult to get out of wood.

Iris wandered about, opening the built-in cupboard and peering into corners. Despite its gory history, it was quite a pleasant room, with a fireplace and an east-facing window.

'You get a nice view from here,' said Violet. 'Not a sea view, but leafy.'

Iris sniffed. 'I DON'T THINK SO.'

'Oh?' said Violet, disappointed. 'Why not?'

'I'M NOT STUPID. I KNOW WHAT HAPPENED IN HERE. COME ON, LIZ, LET'S GO.'

'Why don't you have a cup of tea first, and we can chat about it,' suggested Violet, with a desperate glance at Liz. 'The residents will be having their elevenses downstairs.'

'Tea. Lovely,' said Liz. Maybe she could change Iris's mind. It would take weeks, if not months to sort out Benbow Cottage, and Iris couldn't stay with Irwin that long, not with him sleeping on the floor. Liz would have offered Iris Kipper Cottage, but she had bookings in the diary, and really needed the income to pay for the renovations at Gull.

They joined the residents in the lounge.

'Mrs Gladwell!' Dickie Ledgard jumped up as soon as he saw them. 'Come and sit down.' He offered Iris his chair by the fire, and made Max Plum move along the sofa so he could sit beside him. Patricia, once more in charge of the tea trolley, poured them both a cup.

'NO SUGAR FOR ME. I'M SWEET ENOUGH.'

Dickie chuckled obediently. He was a very personable man, and seemed particularly eager to please Iris.

'Have you been looking at the rooms?' he asked. He had a kind face, that was heavily lined. Liz guessed it was probably from being out all weathers with horses, and the strain of watching his diet for so many years. He was still very slightly built. Liz noticed he didn't take a biscuit himself when he offered them one. Old habits die hard.

'I HAVE,' said Iris, chomping into a biscuit.

'And?' said Patricia. 'Will you be joining us?'

'I DON'T THINK SO.' Iris scattered crumbs as she spoke.

'You didn't like any of the rooms?' asked Patricia. 'I always thought Mr Darnton's room was rather nice.'

'Apart from it being the scene of a recent bloodbath,' chortled Max, clearly thinking he was being witty.

'You can have my room, if you like,' said Dickie to Iris. 'I can move into Roger's.'

'You can't do that!' Max objected. 'Yours is the best room in here. You can't just give it to any old newcomer.'

'WELL, THANKS VERY MUCH,' said Iris.

'I've been here longer,' protested Max. 'I should have first refusal.'

'I'm not offering it to you,' said Dickie mildly. 'I'm offering it to Mrs Gladwell.'

'And Dickie can do what he wants with his room,' chipped in Patricia. 'It's really none of your business, Max, is it?'

'Or yours,' snapped Max. 'Keep your beak out.'

Dickie ignored them both. 'You can come and have a look at it, if you like,' he said to Iris, 'after you've had your tea.'

DICKIE'S ROOM was very nice indeed. Although the large bow window was north-facing, it looked out over the West Cliff promenade and the sea. It was much bigger than any of the rooms they'd seen before, with a rather grand Edwardian fire-

place and elaborate cornice work. The décor was a little tired
and smacked somewhat of the 1980s, with its over-the-top
ruffled pelmet and striped wallpaper, but that didn't seem to
bother Iris. Liz could tell she was impressed.

'IS THIS MUCH MORE EXPENSIVE THAN THE
OTHERS?' she asked.

'I'm not sure, to be honest. I don't know how much the
others are.' Dickie leaned in confidentially. 'But I'm sure that
if you ask nicely, Mrs Baxter will give you a discount.'

Liz thought that was good advice. Violet was desperate to
lease one of her three rooms, and wasn't likely to get many
takers for Clara's or Roger's, not when the Whitby grapevine
was so efficient.

'It's really very nice in summer,' said Dickie. 'You can see
right along the promenade, almost to the whalebone arch.
Excellent for people-watching. Better than the telly, really.'

While Dickie and Iris admired the view, Liz took the
opportunity to look around the rest of the room. It was very
much a bachelor's room, with Dick Francis novels on the
bookcase, racing magazines piled by the bed, and a pipe and
slippers on the hearth. Liz wondered whether Dickie had
ever been married.

She thought his collection of photos might provide the
answer. There were only half a dozen or so scattered among a
collection of silver trophies on the mantelpiece. One photo
was of a much younger, grinning Dickie dressed in racing
silks, his face spattered with mud. There was also a wedding
photo, of Dickie with a dark-haired bride. All the others were
of Dickie and the same woman, taken over several decades.
She had her answer. Dickie Ledgard was presumably a
widower. She looked idly at the trophies. One in particular –
the biggest – caught her eye. To her surprise, the name
engraved on it wasn't Dickie's, but SEAN MCGUIGAN. She
looked at the names on the other cups. Some had RICHARD

LEDGARD on them, but some of the others were engraved with the other name. Liz wondered who Sean McGuigan was, and what Dickie was doing with his trophies.

'If you're interested, Mrs Gladwell, you should move fast. I'm happy to sign the paperwork today, if you like.'

Iris caught Liz's eye. 'WHAT DO YOU THINK, LIZ?'

'I think it's a lovely room, as long Mr Ledgard really doesn't mind?'

Dickie leaned in. 'Sorry, didn't quite catch that. Deaf in one ear, you know.'

'SHE SAID SHE THINKS THE ROOM IS LOVELY. AS LONG AS YOU DON'T MIND MOVING OUT.'

'I don't.' Dickie beamed at them both. 'I can sleep anywhere. And we could do with some new blood in here.' He nudged Iris. 'Shake things up a bit, eh?'

Liz smiled. Iris most definitely would shake things up. She just hoped Dickie knew what he was letting himself in for.

'What do you say, Mrs Gladwell?' Dickie peered at Iris. 'Is it a yes, or a no?'

'YES.'

IRIS DROVE a hard bargain with Violet. It had been almost twelve years since Dickie had signed his lease, but Iris insisted on getting the same deal, plus some knocked off for the cost of redecoration. By the time all the paperwork was signed, Violet looked like a bird that had flown into a plate glass window. Liz felt quite sorry for her, but supposed she had better get used to it – it was just a taste of things to come.

'When will you be moving in?' asked Dickie.

'NO TIME LIKE THE PRESENT. I'LL DO IT TODAY.'

Even Liz was taken aback. 'Don't you want to redecorate first?'

Iris shook her head. 'I CAN'T SPEND ANOTHER MINUTE AT IRWIN'S. HE SNORES SOMETHING SINFUL, YOU KNOW.'

Liz was worried that Irwin would think everything had moved too fast, and that too many decisions had been taken without him. But then she remembered his look of desperation the day before. He would probably be relieved.

'CAN WE FIT EVERYTHING IN YOUR CAR, DO YOU THINK?'

Liz thought about the pile of Iris's things in the café storeroom. 'It might take a few trips, but I'm sure we'll manage.'

IN THE END, it took three trips, each one with Liz's car packed to the roof with Iris's stuff. Tilly and Mags helped Liz load up at the café, while Leah was sent to the Anchorage to help Iris and Dickie at the other end. On her last trip, Liz called into Gull Cottage to take Nelson out for a pee and to see how her tiler was getting on. She was pleased to find he'd already tiled three walls, and was delighted with the effect. The tiles looked even better than she had hoped.

Back at the Anchorage, things were shaping up nicely too. With Leah's help, Iris had made up her bed, and had already unpacked all her clothes into the wardrobe. When Liz arrived, Iris, Dickie and Leah were sitting at the table in the window overlooking the promenade.

'WE SAW YOU COMING,' said Iris gleefully. 'WE CAN SEE EVERYTHING FROM HERE, CAN'T WE, LEAH?'

'We can.'

Liz unpacked her bags. 'I've brought you a few plates, some glasses and some cutlery. I left your pots and pans at the café. I didn't think you would need them here.'

'She won't,' said Dickie. 'We don't do our own cooking. But those glasses will come in handy.' He twinkled at Iris. 'I have a bottle of gin in my new room. Do you fancy a drop, Mrs Gladwell?'

'I DON'T MIND IF I DO, MR LEDGARD.'

Liz saw the opportunity for her and Leah to make their escape.

'We'll leave you to it then,' she said. She shook Dickie's hand. 'Thank you so much. You're a very generous man.'

Dickie frowned. 'Sorry?'

Iris stepped in. 'SHE SAID YOU'RE A GENEROUS MAN.' She addressed Liz. 'HE'S DEAF IN ONE EAR, YOU KNOW.'

'I am.' Dickie nodded. 'But I can always hear you very clearly, Mrs Gladwell.'

18

The following day, Liz planned to grout the bathroom. Leah offered to give her a hand, but Liz wouldn't hear of it.

'Don't be daft,' she said, 'there isn't enough room to swing a cat in there and we'll just get in each other's way. Why don't you go out for the day? Explore. You haven't seen much of the place since you got here.'

She gave Leah the details of buses to Scarborough and the pretty seaside village of Robin Hood's Bay, and prepared herself for her day. Grouting was a boring, mucky job. Liz hated the feel of the grout on her hands as it dried, and so wore disposable surgical gloves. She wore a shower cap, too. She knew she wouldn't be able to have a shower until the grout had dried properly, and she wanted to keep her hair as clean as possible. It was Thursday again. Mah-jong night. She hadn't seen Benedict since he'd sent her the Valentine's card. Would he mention it? She felt a bit giddy just thinking about that. Irritated with herself, she pushed all thoughts of Benedict to one side and got on with the task at hand.

As she expected, it was painstaking, dirty work. She took a break at lunchtime to walk Nelson on Tate Hill beach and to grab a takeaway sandwich from the café. She sat at her kitchen table to eat it, ignoring the pile of Clara's clothes that was still in the corner. (She really *had* to take them to the charity shop!) While she ate, she thought about Iris, and wondered how she was getting on at the Anchorage. She wasn't too worried about her – Dickie Ledgard had been very helpful and attentive. An old-fashioned gentleman. Liz was pretty sure he would do his best to make Iris feel at home. She hoped he'd settled into Roger's room okay, with his photos and trophies. It was strange that some of the trophies were engraved with someone else's name, though. What was it again? Sean McGuigan.

Liz finished her sandwich and pulled her ancient laptop towards her on the table. She fired it up, and it greeted her with its usual 'BONG' that made Nelson jump in his basket. He gave her an accusing look. She ignored him and typed SEAN MCGUIGAN JOCKEY into the search bar.

He had his own Wikipedia page. Sean had been fatally thrown from a horse during a steeplechase in 1978. He was only thirty-two. The article said he had been engaged when he died. It didn't name his fiancée, but there was a picture of them together. Liz peered at the photo of the smiling, dark-haired young woman. She'd seen her face before. Unless she had an identical twin, Sean McGuigan's fiancée was Dickie Ledgard's wife. Had Dickie been friends with Sean? Liz guessed he must have been, because, somehow, he'd ended up with his racing trophies *and* his fiancée. It was all very tragic and fascinating.

But she had work to do! She switched off her laptop, put her dirty dishes in the sink and headed upstairs again.

It was gone half six when she eventually finished. She got to her feet with a groan, and looked around. The delft-style tiles looked beautiful. They were mostly plain with blue corners, but the occasional one had a delicate little sailing ship on it, or a whale. She would still have to give them a final polish to get rid of any traces of grout when everything had dried properly, but she was very, very happy with the result.

She caught her own reflection in the bathroom mirror, and stared at it in dismay. With no make-up and her curly hair – her only real claim to beauty – tucked under the shower cap she looked tired and old. Her chin had a smear of dried grout on it, and her eyes were red with the dust. She looked at her watch and groaned again. She only had half an hour to make herself presentable before going to Benedict's. Perhaps she could just text him and tell him she wasn't going make it? It was very tempting. But then the others wouldn't be able to play Mah-jong. Plus, she knew she was being a coward, running away from Benedict. She lifted her chin to address her reflection in the mirror.

'Get a grip, woman. Sort yourself out.'

So she did. She washed herself as best she could in the bathroom sink, then changed into a green and red sweater dress that she knew made the best of her figure. She brushed her hair vigorously for a few minutes, did her eye make-up and dabbed on some perfume. Ordinarily she'd have worn her ruby studs with that particular dress, but as one was still irritatingly missing, she had to make do with plain gold hoops instead. When she was done she looked at herself critically in her bedroom mirror. Hardly love's young dream. But she would have to do. Her stomach felt a bit queasy

'Yoo hoo!' she heard Niall call as he let himself in downstairs. 'Anyone home?'

Yip!

Liz hurried down the stairs. 'Only me, I'm afraid, and I'm on my way out.'

'Oh yeah, it's Mah-jong night, isn't it? I'd forgotten.' He raised his eyebrows. 'You look nice.'

'Thanks.'

'Do you have any idea where Leah is? She's not answering her phone.'

'She went to Scarborough, I think. On the bus. Or Robin Hood's Bay. Maybe her phone's out of charge?'

'Yeah, that's probably it.'

Liz grabbed her coat. 'Would you mind taking Nelson out? I'm running late.'

'No worries.' He caught her eye and winked. 'Have a grand time.'

KEVIN AND TILLY were already at Benedict's when she arrived. Benedict ushered her in with an anxious look.

'Here you are. I thought you weren't coming.' He helped her out of her coat.

'Yes... um... I've been busy today. Grouting.' She wished she could act naturally with him, but no matter how hard she tried she just couldn't meet his eyes. She saw him frown as he turned away to hang up her coat. Liz could have kicked herself. How old was she? Thirteen? Ridiculous!

'Liz!' Tilly came into the hall and greeted her with a kiss on the cheek and a waft of patchouli oil. 'You look lovely.'

Liz blushed, and followed Benedict and Tilly into the conservatory, where the table was set up for play. Kevin was sitting in one of the bamboo chairs with Delilah the cat on his lap.

'I've just made tapas tonight,' said Benedict. 'We can either eat first, or we can help ourselves as we play, it's up to you.'

'Let's eat now!' said Tilly. 'I'm starving. Also,' she said, casting a sly look at Kevin, 'we can't have Kevin being distracted by food while he's trying to play. He's rubbish enough already.'

Kevin didn't respond with his usual banter. He didn't even acknowledge it. He just stroked Delilah with a distracted air. Liz wondered what he was so preoccupied about.

Everyone helped themselves to tapas from the sideboard, and sat at the table with their plates. Benedict poured them each a glass of wine.

'So,' said Tilly to Kevin. 'Tell us what's been happening in the thrilling world of law enforcement?'

Kevin shrugged. 'Not much.'

'Really?' Tilly was surprised.

Liz couldn't blame her. With two murder investigations on the go, it was hard to believe Kevin wasn't rushed off his feet. He saw their scepticism.

'I broke up a disturbance of the peace this morning,' he said.

Liz guessed he was deflecting from any discussion of the murders.

'Oh?' Tilly was intrigued. 'Who disturbed the peace?'

'Rose Young.'

Liz frowned. 'Rose Young the fortune teller?'

Kevin nodded. 'She got into an argument with someone up at East Terrace. Threw a rock through their window.'

'A rock?' Liz found that hard to believe, too. 'Whose window?'

'That woman who's into all the woo-woo stuff. You know... spiritualism. Blakey.'

Tilly's eyes widened. 'Isn't that where you went to the séance? The Third Eye Society?'

Liz nodded. She hadn't known that Hilda Blakey and Rose knew each other. 'What was the argument about?'

'No idea. Neither of the women would tell me. But they were both in a fair old state. I managed to calm everything down without hauling them both to the station. They were lucky it was me who picked up the call. If it had been a uniform, they'd have been in trouble.'

Liz ate her tapas in thoughtful silence. Rose Young hadn't seemed the sort of person to lose her temper easily – she'd kept her cool even when Dora and her cohorts were besieging her kiosk. So what on earth could have riled her so badly that she'd thrown a rock through a window?

'I think we should make a start,' said Benedict, when they'd finished eating. 'We don't want to be here all night. Liz, can you give me a hand with the plates, into the kitchen?'

Liz, pulled from her musings about Hilda and Rose, helped him clear the table. They scraped the plates in the bin in the kitchen, and put them in the sink. They did it in silence, but out of the corner of her eye she could see Benedict darting glances at her.

'How are you?' he asked at last.

'Fine.'

'Did you have a good Valentine's day?'

'Great, thanks.' They smiled at each other, awkward, and the conversation dried up again. Liz cursed herself. She didn't know what was wrong with her. She really was acting like a tongue-tied teenager.

They headed back to the conservatory, through the hall.

'Hang on a minute.' Benedict stopped her. 'Your label's sticking out.'

'Is it?' Liz put her hand to the back of her neck.

'Let me tuck it in for you.' He reached around her to tuck the label of her dress back in. He was very close.

She kissed him.

His lips were firm under hers, and she could smell his skin. He smelled of soap, and lemons, and tapas spices. There was a second of frozen surprise, then he kissed her back. After a blissful moment of pleasure, she broke away.

'Oh my God. I'm so sorry.' She hadn't thought before she'd done it. She'd just... done it. And now she was mortified.

'What on earth are you sorry for?' Benedict grinned at her. 'That was lovely. I was going to kiss you, the other night when I walked you home, but then Niall opened the door. I could have wrung his neck.'

He kissed her again, this time rather more thoroughly, bringing blood rushing to her face and to other parts of her she'd almost completely forgotten about. She could feel the warmth of him through her clothes, on her skin...

BANG BANG! RIIIIING!

They broke apart.

'Are you all in there?' They recognised Niall's voice, and could see the shape of him through the glass in the front door. 'Open up, Benedict!'

Benedict closed his eyes and groaned. 'I swear to God, that lad is a romance repellent!'

He went to open the front door anyway, leaving Liz bereft.

Niall charged into the hall. 'Is Leah here?'

'No,' said Benedict. 'Why would she be?'

'She still hasn't turned up at Gull. I've tried everywhere. I'm really worried. We made plans to go out tonight, but she hasn't even called. She's not picking up her phone either.'

Tilly and Kevin had come out of the conservatory to see what the noise was about. Liz smoothed her hair and wondered if her face looked as flushed as it felt. She hoped she didn't look as if she'd just been kissed.

'Have you tried the café?' asked Tilly

'Yeah. Mags hasn't seen her.'

'What about Iris, up at the Anchorage?' suggested Liz.

Niall looked relieved and slapped himself on the forehead. 'I forgot she'd moved! I went to Neptune Yard, but of course there was nobody there... Iris doesn't have a mobile, does she? I'll head up there now.'

'No.' Kevin stopped him before he got back to the door. 'Don't waste your time. Leah's not at the Anchorage.'

Everyone looked at him.

'She's at the station.'

19

'**B**ut why?' demanded Niall. 'Why would you arrest Leah?'

Kevin saw their shocked expressions and realised he was going to have to explain. 'Because of the DNA, from the epithelials we found under Clara's fingernails. We had to take DNA from Clara, to rule out the possibility that she'd scratched herself. The epithelial DNA didn't match Clara's. Not exactly. But it was a close match. It could only have come from a relative.'

'No way.' Niall shook his head furiously. 'Leah wasn't even in the country when Clara was murdered. She was in Nepal. She can prove it. Check with the airline. Check with Passport Control.'

Kevin gave him a sorrowful look. 'We did. Leah flew back to the UK three days before Clara died.'

Niall sat down heavily on one of the hall chairs.

No one spoke for a long moment.

'There has to be a logical explanation,' said Liz, eventually.

'Are you sure?' said Kevin. 'How well do we know Leah? Any of us?'

'I do,' said Niall. 'I know her.'

'Really?' said Kevin. 'You've only...'

'Shut up!' said Niall. 'Just... don't say it.'

Kevin didn't say it. No one else spoke either, digesting the shocking news.

Niall was the first to break the silence. He glared at Kevin.

'I can't believe you knew and you didn't say anything.' His face was expressionless. 'Why didn't you say anything?'

'I didn't know it was going to happen tonight,' protested Kevin. 'I've been trying to persuade Flint to be cautious, to be sure of our facts before we made the arrest. But obviously, she's taken advantage of the fact it's my night off.'

'To be fair,' cut in Benedict. 'Kevin really couldn't say anything, could he? He can't share an ongoing investigation with all and sundry. He'd be putting his job on the line.'

'On the line, my arse,' snapped Niall. He headed for the door again.

Benedict stepped towards him. 'Come on, Niall, you're not being fair.'

Niall ignored him and slammed out.

Liz turned to Benedict. 'He's in love with the girl.' She grabbed her coat. 'Fair doesn't come into it.'

'Niall! Slow down!' Liz caught up with him about fifty yards down the street. 'Where are you going?'

'The police station.'

'Okay... but don't go crashing in there, all guns blazing. Calm down.' Liz knew she was risking Flint's wrath by tagging along, but she couldn't let Niall go on his own.

Niall stopped walking. 'She didn't kill her, Liz.' In the light of the nearby street lamp Liz could see his eyes were unnaturally bright. 'I know she didn't.'

She patted his arm, resisting the urge to hug him. 'I'm sure you're right. There'll be an explanation, I'm sure.'

'I've never had much luck with women. God knows, I haven't had much luck with anything else either. But I thought... this time...' He dashed a tear away with his hand, angry with himself.

Liz gave in to her urge and pulled him into a hug. They stood like that for a minute or so, as she tried to infuse him with some of her strength. Eventually, she stepped back.

'Come on. Let's go see what's happening.'

At the sound of a car engine, they both turned. Kevin's car pulled up to the kerb beside them. Niall ignored it, and set off walking again. Not knowing what else to do, Liz trotted after him.

The car followed them both. Kevin wound his window down.

'Don't be an arsehole, Niall,' he called out. 'Get in. I'll take you there.'

But the young Irishman kept walking with Liz scurrying along beside him.

Kevin didn't give up. 'Don't you think you have a better chance of finding out what's going on if I'm there? A better chance of getting Leah out?'

Niall stopped to digest this. After a moment's inner debate, he reached for the passenger door handle and got in, without saying anything.

Liz climbed into the back seat.

They drove in silence. When they got to the station at Spring Hill, Niall jumped straight out as soon as Kevin pulled into a parking space. Liz started to get out, too, but Kevin stopped her.

'I'm not being funny, but I think you'd better stay in the

car. You're like a red rag to a bull with Flint. You're not going to help us in there.'

Liz knew he was right.

They watched through the windscreen as Niall marched into the station. Kevin swore under his breath. 'Talking about bulls, there's one charging into a china shop.' He turned back to Liz. 'I'll come and let you know what's going on as soon as I can, okay?'

Liz nodded. 'Look after him.'

'I'll do my best.' Kevin got out of the car and disappeared into the station after Niall.

Liz was left on her own. She really hoped the police were wrong, and Leah had nothing to do with Clara's murder, but she couldn't see how they could be. How did Leah's skin get under Clara's fingernails? And why did Leah lie about when she'd flown back from Nepal? Liz felt terrible for Niall. He had fallen hard. It would be devastating for him to lose Leah so soon after finding her.

That thought led, inevitably, to Benedict. And the kiss. That kiss! She could still feel the warmth of his lips on hers. She couldn't believe she'd just kissed him totally out of the blue! It hadn't been bravery, but pure, animal instinct. She hadn't had a thought in her head when she'd done it. It was marvellous. Exhilarating. And yet...

And yet.

If she was honest, now she had some distance, she had to admit there had been something... off... about it. On the one hand it had been lovely, but on the other, it had just felt... wrong. It had been more than five years since she'd kissed anyone, and longer since she'd kissed anyone with passion – Mark was ill for a long time before he died. She supposed it wasn't really surprising she felt so conflicted about the prospect of kissing – and potentially sleeping with – someone else. *Sleeping with.* Just the thought of being intimate with a man was terrifying, even it was Benedict. She shivered.

She pulled her coat more tightly around herself. It was getting pretty cold. She looked at the dashboard, wondering if she could turn the ignition to get the heater working, but Kevin had taken the keys into the station with him.

After another ten minutes or so, her teeth began to chatter. It was February, for heaven's sake! No one would leave a *dog* in an unheated car in February. She got out of the car, and went into the station.

Reception was empty apart from an anxious-looking middle-aged couple, sitting in silence, staring at the ceiling. There was nobody behind the counter. Liz slid onto one of the plastic chairs, hoping that no one would notice her there. She was now dangerously in Flint's orbit, but at least she was warming up. It took her ten minutes to stop shaking.

It was another half an hour before the door into the station opened, and Niall came out, with Kevin behind him. Niall's whole body language had changed. An air of intense defeat hung over him like a cloud. The contrast with the belligerent way he'd gone into the station reminded Liz of the saying about the month of March – 'going in like a lion and coming out like a lamb.'

They all got in the car. Nobody spoke.

'Well,' prompted Liz, finally, from the back seat. 'What's going on?'

'Leah's still being interviewed,' said Kevin. 'We watched some of it through the one-way mirror.'

'Are you supposed to do that?' asked Liz.

Kevin snorted. 'Flint would have my balls if she knew I'd taken him in there.' He glanced at Niall. 'But I had some bridges to build.'

'So...?' prompted Liz again.

Kevin continued. 'Leah's denying she had anything to do with Clara's death.' He hesitated. 'She does have an explanation for lying about when she was back in the country.' He shot another anxious look at Niall, who roused himself enough to speak.

'She was with a man,' he said. 'They were holed up in a hotel in London. She hadn't wanted to explain all that to the police, or explain why she hadn't answered any of their calls.' He lifted his chin. 'It was none of their business, anyway.'

He was right. It wasn't. But Liz was relieved.

'That's great, though, isn't it?' she said. 'The man can give her an alibi.'

'It isn't as easy as that,' said Kevin. He glanced anxiously at Niall again.

Niall looked grim. 'He's married. Leah won't give Flint his name.'

'Ah.'

'She won't even give us the name of the hotel she was staying in,' said Kevin. 'I suppose she knows we'll be able to track him down from the hotel records. But... the upshot is, she has no alibi. Combined with the DNA evidence we already have, that doesn't look good.'

'So what happens now?' asked Liz.

'We'll send her DNA sample to the lab, obviously, to check it's exactly the same as the DNA under Clara's fingernails. But that could take a while. In the meantime, we'll check CCTV at the train and bus stations. See if we can spot her arriving in Whitby in the time frame of the murder.'

Niall glared at him.

Kevin had the grace to blush. 'She'll have a lawyer assigned to her, and they'll post bail.'

'Will she get it?'

'Probably. As long as someone stumps up the cash. Unless

we...' he corrected himself, '... unless *someone* finds enough evidence to make us think she's likely to do a runner.'

Niall snorted. 'How can she do a runner if you have her passport?'

'She could run off to somewhere in the UK, couldn't she? Scotland... Wales?'

'Whatever.' Niall was unimpressed by Kevin's suggestions. 'Can we please go home now?'

They all drove back to Gull Cottage without speaking. Niall jumped out of the car as soon as it stopped, and let himself in. Liz smiled ruefully at Kevin.

'Thanks,' she said. 'Try not to feel too bad about it.'

'I don't feel bad about it, not really. I feel sorry for him, obviously, but if Leah *is* a murderer...'

'You have to do your job.'

'Exactly. Give me a ring in the morning. Let me know how he is.'

'Will do.' She hurried after Niall.

When she got indoors, she took off her coat and hung it up. Niall was petting Nelson half-heartedly. He looked up at her. 'I don't understand, Liz. I don't understand why she didn't tell me about this bloke in London.'

'She probably would have done, eventually. It was still early days for you both, wasn't it? There's a good chance she just didn't want you to think less of her. When you're just starting out, you want to make the best possible impression.'

Niall didn't look convinced.

'And,' continued Liz, 'I think it says a lot about her, that she isn't prepared to dump this man in it – ruin his marriage – to save her own skin.'

'Suppose.' He rubbed a hand wearily over his face. 'I'm away to my bed now, if you don't mind?'

'Of course not.'

Her heart went out to him as he trudged up the stairs.

Liz clipped Nelson on his lead and took him out for his last walk of the day. Tate Hill beach was dark, the only illumination coming from the lights of the harbour opposite and their reflections on the water. Liz sighed and pulled her coat more tightly around her as she crunched over the pebbles. She was beyond weary. Beyond thought, apart from putting one foot in front of the other. She surrendered to the here and now, to the sound of her crunching feet and the waves lapping the shore, the scent of brine and seaweed.

When she got home again, she settled Nelson for the night and headed up to her own bed.

She lay in the darkness, listening to the silence. There was no sound at all from the street, and no murmuring voices from Niall's room below. Niall was convinced Leah wasn't a murderer, and Liz really, really wanted to trust his judgement. He might not be physically related to her, but he felt like family. Like a son, or a much younger brother.

Liz sat up suddenly. Adrenalin sparked through her veins. *Could it be?*

It was unlikely. The longest of long shots. Mad, even! But, if Niall's instincts were right – and she really hoped they were – there *could* be another explanation for the evidence against Leah.

20

'Have you lost your tiny little mind?' squeaked Kevin over the phone.

'It's the only possible explanation.'

'No, it isn't.'

'I don't think Leah killed Clara. Niall doesn't either.'

'You're letting your fondness for him cloud your judgement.'

'I still think you should suggest it to Flint as a possibility.'

'Me? I'm not going to do that. She'll think I've gone round the bend.'

'Then I'll do it. She thinks I'm round the bend already.'

'She might be right.' Kevin tried a more reasonable tone. 'You can't be serious, Liz.'

'I'm deadly serious. If you don't want to get caught in the fallout, make yourself scarce at the station this morning. I won't hold it against you.'

. . .

NIALL CALLED in sick again to work, so Liz left Nelson in his
care. She didn't tell him where she was going, or what she
planned to do. He had enough to worry about.

The walk to Spring Hill was almost enjoyable, in spite of
her mission. The winter sunlight sparkled on the sea, and
seagulls swooped overhead. When Liz arrived at the ugly
brick police station, she hesitated. Was this really a good
idea? Was Kevin right? Was she out of her mind? It was a
possibility, but she didn't see she had much choice. She lifted
her chin and walked in.

The waiting room was busier than it had been the night
before.

'Please just wait your turn, Mr Calder.' Constable
Williams was on duty at the counter, dealing with a member
of the public, an old man in a flat cap.

'I'm telling you, he bloody well cut it down,' yelled the old
man. 'Look at this! Just look at it!'

It was impossible not to. He was brandishing what
seemed to be the greater part of a massive bush, shaking it so
its leaves scattered over the scuffed vinyl floor.

'I can see it, Mr Calder,' said Williams, unruffled. 'We can
all see it. If you'll take a seat, I'll attend to you – and your
bush – when it's your turn.'

There were several other people already perched on the
plastic chairs, watching. One of them, a youth in his late
teens, was grinning from ear to ear, enjoying the floor show.

'What are you laughing at?' The old man turned on him.
'This is a serious business. Vandalism!' He brandished the
bush threateningly at the youth, who just laughed.

Liz made the most of the distraction to sidle up to the
counter. Williams spotted her and his eyes widened in
surprise.

'Mrs Mac.'

'A quiet day at the office?' she asked, ironic.

'Same old, same old.' He gave her a doleful smile. 'What can I do for you?'

'Is DI Flint in? I really need to speak to her.'

'Really?'

''Fraid so.'

'OW! OW!' The youth howled, as the old man started thrashing him with the bush. 'GERROF ME, YOU OLD LOONY!'

'Oh, for the love of God,' muttered Williams. He disappeared from behind the counter, and reappeared a moment later through the internal door. He rushed to intercede.

'Mr Calder! Mr Calder! Stop it!'

The old man either didn't hear him, or didn't want to. He continued to thrash the youth, who was now rolling on the floor, cackling with laughter. Most of the other people in the waiting room were laughing, too, or trying not to.

'I'll teach you to take the piss out of me, you little beggar.' The old man was bright red in the face.

'Mr Calder.' Williams tried to catch his arm. 'Stop. That's enough, or you'll give yourself a heart attack.'

'WHAT IN GOD'S NAME IS GOING ON IN HERE?' The voice boomed around the waiting room.

Everyone froze.

DI Flint stood in the doorway, hands on hips, glaring at the scene in front of her. When she spotted Liz, her eyes widened. Ignoring the old man, the bush, the youth cowering on the floor, and Constable Williams, she addressed Liz.

'I might have known.'

Williams frowned, 'But Mrs Mac didn't have anything—'

Flint silenced him with a glare and pointed at Liz. 'You,' she said. 'Come with me.' She turned on her heel and strode back the way she'd come.

Liz followed, pulling a rueful face at Williams, who was clearly appalled by the turn of events. Liz wasn't particularly happy either. It didn't bode well for the already tricky conversation she knew was coming.

Flint led the way through the corridors to an interview room. It was one Liz had been in before.

'Sit,' said Flint, as if she was speaking to a dog.

Liz sat. Flint took the seat opposite her and folded her arms.

'Speak.'

'I came in to—'

'Why is it,' cut in Flint, 'that whenever there is a fracas of some sort, I always find you in the middle of it?'

Liz opened her mouth to reply, but Flint cut her off again.

'I'll tell you why. It's because you are an agent of chaos.'

Liz's eyes widened. That was a bit much.

'I really don't—'

'An agent of discord and confusion. Whitby's very own Loki, in fact.'

Liz didn't know what to say to that. She thought it best to ignore it. 'I have some information.'

'About?'

'Clara Bendelow's murder.'

A smile crept across Flint's sharp features. A genuine smile. It quite unnerved Liz. But she kept going.

'Leah didn't kill Clara. There is another explanation for the familial DNA you found under Clara's fingernails. Her brother, Eddie. I think he killed her.'

Flint nodded. 'This is the same brother who killed himself in 1989?'

Liz nodded. 'I don't think he did, though.'

'Okay. So... if Eddie Bendelow is still alive, where's he been for the last thirty years?' She paused for dramatic effect. 'Living with Elvis and Bigfoot on the Yellow Submarine?' Her lips twitched at her own wit.

'I know it sounds far-fetched.'

'If you have evidence, I will consider it.' She smiled at Liz. 'You do have evidence?'

She took Liz's silence as her answer.

'In my experience, Mrs McLuckie... my *considerable* experience... the simplest, most straightforward explanation is usually the right one. We have our murderer. It's only a matter of time before we have all the evidence we need to convict her.'

'I don't think you're going to find it. Leah was in—'

'You know what?' Flint rose to her feet. 'I'm not prepared to discuss the ins and outs of the case with you.' She grinned. 'Elizabeth McLuckie, I'm arresting you for obstruction of justice. You do not have to say anything. But, it may harm your defence if you do not mention when questioned something which you later rely on in court. Anything you do say may be given in evidence.'

LIZ STARED AT THE CEILING. It had a crack that ran diagonally from two of the opposite corners, and a large yellow stain the size of a carrier bag almost in the centre. She'd had quite a lot of time to consider the source of the stain, and had come to the conclusion it was probably from a leaky roof. The holding cells were in a single-storey extension at the back of the building. As the station had been built in the 1970s, Liz thought there was a good chance it had a flat roof. Flat roofs were notorious for leaks. Liz was something of an expert on leaking roofs, although hers were eighteenth-century slate ones rather than flat felted ones.

Having exhausted the entertainment potential of the ceiling for the umpteenth time, Liz's eyes moved back to the window, set high in the wall, where a spider had started to spin a web across the bars. It had progressed quite a lot since she'd started watching it, and had now reached the third bar.

Liz had no idea how long that had taken, as she'd had to surrender her watch, phone and shoes to the sergeant at the processing desk. She watched the spider as it spun its web, impressed with its agility and persistence. It reminded her of the tales of her countryman, King Robert the Bruce, after his defeat at the hands of the English...

Her thoughts were interrupted by the sound of feet approaching along the corridor. Two pairs – one heavy, one lighter. Thanks to Constable's Williams's intervention, she'd managed to make her single phone call before she was processed. She hadn't wanted to call Kevin, because she didn't want to compromise him, nor had she called Tilly, given her track record with the police. Benedict was out of the question, so that had left only one possibility...

The footsteps stopped at her door, and the key turned in the lock. The door swung open, and Patricia Haddington stood in the doorway.

'Who's been a naughty girl?' She crossed her arms under her tweedy bosom.

Liz stood up. 'I'm really sorry I bothered you,' she said. 'I don't know any other solicitors.'

'Fret not.' Patricia arched one eyebrow. 'We'll have you out of here in two shakes of a lamb's tail.'

IT TOOK A SLIGHTLY LONGER than that, but not much. Patricia started their meeting with Flint by pointing out that actually there was no such charge as obstruction of justice. It was actually *perverting* the course of justice, and was usually only applicable in a courtroom situation. She continued by arguing that, as there was no malicious intent, any charge was likely to be refused anyway, which wouldn't reflect well on DI Flint. Flint didn't want to get on the wrong side of the CPS or the DPP, did she?

Flint sat smirking throughout. When Patricia had finished, she didn't look at all cowed by her eloquence.

'Okay,' she said, with an unconcerned shrug. 'She can go.'

Patricia frowned. 'There is such a thing as wrongful arrest, you know.'

'There is,' acknowledged Flint. 'But I don't think you'll be pushing your luck that far. In order to practise law, a solicitor has to keep up with their certification. Have you kept up with your certification, Mrs Haddington?'

Patricia scowled. '*Ms* Haddington.'

Flint stood up. 'Let's just call it quits, shall we, *Ms* Haddington?'

When Patricia had left, Flint followed Liz to the processing counter and watched as she retrieved her things. Liz guessed she'd never intended the charge to stick. She'd just wanted to scare her.

Liz smiled brightly at Flint as she went out. If she wanted to frighten her, she'd have to try harder than that!

She got a certain amount of satisfaction from seeing something flicker on Flint's face. Dismay? Or irritation? Liz was happy, either way.

NIALL WAS WAITING for her outside, in Frannie the Fiat.

'Kevin called me,' he said, by way of explanation, 'and told me what was happening. I thought you might like a lift.'

They headed home to the east side.

'So DI Flint wasn't impressed with your theory?' he said as they waited for the signal at the bridge.

'Not very.' Liz sighed. 'Can't say I blame her, really.'

The barrier went up, and they drove in silence for another few moments.

'Thank you,' said Niall.

Liz looked at him.

'Thank you for believing me. All this business with the bloke in London really doesn't make any difference. I know Leah didn't do it.' He paused. 'I haven't known her long, but the thing is... sometimes you just click with people, don't you? She's one of the most honest people I know.'

Liz nodded. 'In that case, Eddie Bendelow is the only possible explanation.'

'Agreed.' Niall pulled a face. 'But how do we find him?'

21

St Mary's church bell woke Liz the next morning. As soon as she heard it clang six o'clock, she jumped out of bed. By seven o'clock, she'd already given Nelson his morning walk, done the cleaning and laundry changeover at Kipper Cottage, and put some coffee on the stove. She opened her door just as Mike Howson was passing.

'Mrs Mac!' He clutched his heart in mock fright. 'You made me jump there.' He sniffed the air. 'Is that coffee I can smell?'

'Time for a quick one?'

'Is the Pope Catholic?' He beamed. 'Give me a minute to drop these off.'

He continued with his box of herring to the smokehouse next door, while Liz busied herself making two mugs of coffee. She'd been thinking about Eddie Bendelow, and where he could possibly be. Somehow Clara's killer had managed to get into the Anchorage, find her room, and get out again without being seen. It was likely he knew his way around the place. Could he be living there under a different name? Could he be Max Plum? Or even Dickie Ledgard?

It was a bizarre thought, but not impossible. Three decades had passed since Eddie's supposed death. He was likely to have changed a lot in that time. Mike had said he knew Dickie, and he liked to talk, which made him the perfect place to start her process of elimination.

There was a knock at the door.

'It's open!'

Mike came in, bringing with him, as always, the aroma of fish. Liz really didn't mind. His herring were always freshly caught, and smelled of the sea rather than anything unpleasant. He took off his hat and high-vis vest, and rubbed his red cheeks.

'Nice and warm in here,' he said, approvingly. 'You got your heating sorted, then?'

Liz nodded. 'Just everything else to sort out now.'

'Expensive business, renovating.'

'Did you hear about Iris's cottage?' she asked, steering the conversation.

'No?'

'Her ceiling came down. A leak.'

'Poor love. And her with her dicky heart and all.'

Liz hurried to reassure him. 'She's fine. She's moved into the Anchorage. Dickie Ledgard gave her his room.'

'Dickie's a gent.'

'He is, isn't he? He's a widower, I take it?' She already knew he was, but had to start somewhere.

Mike nodded. 'His wife, Ellen, has been dead for... it must be about ten years now.'

'Wasn't she engaged to one of his friends, before she married him?'

'Aye, Sean McGuigan. He was killed in a race at York, you know. Horrible. Three horses went down, only two riders got up. Ellen was his fiancée... she was in a terrible state. Everyone was relieved when Dickie took her under his wing. We all thought she was better off with Dickie anyway.'

'Why's that?'

Mike didn't need much prompting to keep going. 'Between you and me, Mrs Mac, Sean had his problems. Gambling. And the drink. Turned out, Dickie was a much safer bet. Him and Ellen had just celebrated their pearl anniversary when she died.'

'You've known him a long time, then?'

'He was at school with my older brother, Ned. We all grew up together.'

Which meant that Dickie couldn't be Eddie. Liz was relieved. She'd liked what she'd seen of Dickie Ledgard. She sipped her coffee thoughtfully.

'Do you know Max Plum at all? He's at the Anchorage, too.'

'Is that the fella from Middlesbrough?'

'I don't know where he's from.'

'I think he is. Lived on one of the rougher estates. Had a run-in with a neighbour from hell. Probably thought the Anchorage would be a safe haven.' Mike snorted. 'Out of the frying pan into the fire.'

Some of what Mike said surprised Liz. Max had a posh accent. Southern. He certainly didn't sound like he came from Middlesbrough. But she wasn't so surprised to learn he'd had a run-in with a neighbour. He was certainly argumentative enough. Could he be Eddie Bendelow? He was about the right age, and might be putting on the accent to disguise his identity. But... Liz suddenly realised there was a serious flaw in her whole line of investigation. Surely Clara would have recognised her own brother? Especially if she was seeing him every day at the Anchorage? Eddie would have changed, but surely not *that* much? She sighed. Perhaps she had to think again.

. . .

WHEN MIKE HAD GONE, Liz finished her coffee. There'd been no sign of Niall that morning, which wasn't particularly surprising, as it was a Saturday. She couldn't imagine he'd slept well. She made some toast, fried some bacon and scrambled some eggs, then took them upstairs on a tray with a mug of tea. She tapped on Niall's door, telling herself that if he was still asleep, she'd take them down again. But she got an answer straight away.

'Yeah?' His voice through the door wasn't at all sleepy.

'Can I come in?'

'Hang on a sec.' There was some rustling inside the room. 'Okay. All decent.'

Niall was propped up in bed with his hair sticking up and his duvet tucked around him. There were shadows under his eyes.

'Is that bacon I can smell?' he asked hopefully.

'And scrambled egg.'

'You're a star!' He took the tray like a starving man. 'Sit down, why don't you? I could do with some company.'

As if hearing his words there was a scrabble at the door, and Nelson barged his way in. He jumped up onto the bed.

'Bad dog!' Liz went to lift him off, but Niall stopped her.

'Leave him, he's grand. Aren't you, boy?' He scratched him under the chin. Nelson grinned at her, tongue lolling. Knowing she was outnumbered, Liz perched on the bed beside them.

'How did you sleep?' she asked.

'I didn't. All I can think about is Leah in a police cell.'

'Try not to worry about her. She probably bunked down in some pretty tough places in Nepal.'

'Probably.' Niall fed Nelson a chunk of bacon. Liz pretended not to see.

'So,' he said, 'what next? Do we have a plan of action?'

'First of all, we need to find out how much Leah's bail is likely to be.'

Niall's face fell. 'Sure, I'd forgotten about that. It's going to be thousands, isn't it?' He brightened again. 'Maybe we can use her inheritance from Clara?'

'I don't think so. She's just been accused of murdering her. The CPS will freeze the cash, if they haven't already.'

'So where will we get the money?'

'One step at a time. Leah should have been given legal representation by now. Can you find out who it is, and get in touch with them? Ask how much her bail is likely to be?'

'I'll head up to the station as soon as I'm dressed.' Niall looked at her. 'What about you? What will you be doing?'

'I'm going to find Eddie Bendelow.'

THE OFFICES of the *Whitby Bugle* were on Flowergate, above the Yorkshire Rose Building Society. In the days before the digital age, the building used to be filled with the clatter of printing presses, and the smell of ink. But now it was much the same as any other open-plan office. During the week, it was busy with phones ringing and people milling around, but it was much quieter on Saturdays, with only one receptionist at the desk.

Liz paid her research fee, and the receptionist took her through to the microfiche room. Anything after the year 2000 had been digitised, but everything before that was only accessible on microfiche. Liz guessed she had a long morning ahead of her.

She was right. It took her more than two hours to trawl through the 1989 editions of the newspaper to find the one that covered Eddie Bendelow's apparent suicide, that was dated 6th October. It was just a two-paragraph piece, that gave only the barest of details – the fact he'd been missing for three weeks, that his clothes had been found on the West Cliff beach, and that his family had been notified. There was a brief comment from the RNLI station commander, about the strength and unpredictability of the tides and the likelihood of the body being recovered (extremely slim). There was no photograph.

Liz kept looking. More than an hour later, she found the report on the coroner's verdict of accidental death, given on the basis that Eddie had left no suicide note. Again, there was no photograph.

Liz switched the machine off and rubbed her aching neck. She'd drawn a blank. Thanks to the *Bugle's* unexpectedly discreet reporting, there were no clues as to what Eddie's motive for faking his suicide might have been, and not a single photograph. She still had no idea what Eddie even looked like.

Liz remembered Clara's shoebox. Could there be a photograph of Eddie in it? She didn't remember taking the box to the Anchorage with Iris's other things, so it was either still at Benbow Cottage, or Iris had thrown it out. And she didn't think Iris would have thrown it out.

She set off for the east side, stiff from having sat so long in one position, her eyes sore from peering at the microfiche. As she passed the Full Moon Café, she glanced inside, and was startled to see Benedict sitting at a table beside the window. He looked up just as Liz passed. Liz ducked her head and put on a burst of speed. She darted into the glass workshop a few doors down, and stepped behind someone who was looking at the rainbow displays of Lucky Ducks. Benedict passed the shop at speed seconds later, scanning the crowd ahead of him with a frown. Liz gave it a few minutes before she ventured out again, and cut quickly down to Tate Hill beach. She didn't want to risk bumping into him again on Church Street.

She wasn't sure why she was avoiding him. With every-thing else that had been going on, she hadn't had the time to process their kiss properly, or to work out why it had felt so awkward. She knew it was cowardly, but she really didn't want to have to talk to him until she'd worked out what was going on in her own head. She had thought she'd wanted a romance – been desperate for it, even – but now she wasn't sure.

THE DOOR of Benbow Cottage was open when she got to Neptune Yard. There were several black bin bags outside, filled to bursting with debris. She stuck her head into the hall.

'Hello?' she called.

'Hello?' An answer came back from somewhere inside, and seconds later an outlandish figure appeared, dressed entirely in blue plastic, features hidden by a surgical face mask and plastic work goggles.

Irwin took off the goggles. They left pressure marks around his eyes like a panda.

'Sorry if I gave you a fright,' he said. 'I borrowed this forensic suit from Kevin. I'm just trying to clear up some of the mess.'

She followed him into the kitchen, where he'd been scraping up the sludgy remains of the ceiling, and shovelling them into bin bags. It was dirty, unpleasant work, but didn't totally warrant Irwin's take-no-chances sartorial approach.

'Can I give you a hand?' Liz felt she should offer.

'I don't have another suit.'

'That's okay. These are my work clothes anyway.'

After they'd wrangled the broken, sodden plaster into bin bags, they scrubbed all the surfaces with warm soapy water and swabbed the floor. When they'd finished, the cottage looked much, much better, even though they could still see right up to the roof through the beams.

'When is the insurance company coming?' asked Liz.

'Monday,' said Irwin. 'I'm not sure they'll pay out, given it was mother's fault and not an actual leak.'

'Let's keep our fingers crossed.' Liz suddenly remembered why she'd come to Neptune Yard in the first place. 'I don't suppose you've come across Clara Bendelow's box of photos while you were clearing up?'

'The old Clarks shoebox?'

Liz nodded.

Irwin pulled a face. 'I had to bin it. It was just a mushed-up mess.'

'Oh.'

He saw her expression. 'Sorry. Was there something important in it?'

'I doubt it.' She squashed down her disappointment, and realised she was thirsty. 'You know what, I could do with a beer. I have some in the fridge at Gull. Do you fancy one before you head home?'

Irwin brightened. 'I don't mind if I do.'

ALTHOUGH NELSON CAME to greet them in Gull Cottage, there was no sign of Niall. Liz guessed he was still carrying out his part of their mission. She hoped he was having more success than she was.

Irwin shrugged himself out of his plastic overalls at the door. Under his plastic suit, he was immaculately dressed in a tweed three-piece suit and a shirt and tie. Liz had never seen him in anything that could remotely be called casual, apart from the snazzy jumpers he liked to wear at Christmas.

Liz found the beer in the fridge and poured one for them both.

'Cheers,' said Irwin, clinking his glass against hers. '*Let us drink down all unkindness.*'

Prior to becoming a mortuary make-up artist, Irwin had worked in the theatre. His theatrical tendencies still occasionally slipped out.

They both turned as they heard a scratching noise. It was Nelson, grubbing at the pile of Clara's old clothes that lay in the corner. Liz suffered a flash of guilt – she still hadn't taken them to the charity shop.

'Leave it, Nelson.'

But Nelson wouldn't leave the clothes alone. He continued to scratch, until he uncovered his target – a checked skirt with floral trim. He picked it up and carried it to Liz, like a gun dog presenting a rabbit.

'I'm not sure that's really your style,' said Irwin, with a smile.

'Me neither.' She returned the skirt to the pile.

'How's your mum settling in at the Anchorage?' she asked, as she took her seat again.

'Marvellously well. I don't know quite how you managed it, but thank you.'

Nelson trotted over to the pile of clothes again, picked up the skirt and brought it back to Liz. He dropped it at her feet, and looked at her expectantly.

'I don't want it. Whatever's got into you?'

'He seems very taken with it.'

'He does, doesn't he?' She picked it up again, to return it to the pile. As she did, she felt something small and hard through the material. Something in the pocket. She pulled it out.

'What is it?' asked Irwin.

'A necklace.' She inspected it more closely. 'A locket.' She held it up for him to see. It was oval, made of gold, with a fine gold chain.

'Didn't you check the pockets?' asked Irwin.

'Leah did. Not too well, obviously. This is the second thing I've found.'

'It looks quite valuable, doesn't it? Clever dog!'

'The chain's broken,' said Liz. 'Maybe Clara put it in her pocket when it broke.'

Liz opened the locket. There were two faded colour photographs inside, facing each other. One was Clara, and the other was a young man. The photograph was small, but Liz could see he was clean-shaven, with a shock of sandy hair and a pale complexion. She peered closer, and caught her breath.

Eddie Bendelow had changed – a lot.

But she still recognised him.

22

Liz took a deep breath, and rang the bell. After a little while, she heard movement inside the house, and the front door opened.

Graham stood on the doorstep, wearing his floral apron. He frowned when he saw Liz.

'You've just missed her,' he said.

'I haven't come to see Hilda. It's you I want to talk to.'

He scratched his beard. 'What about?'

'It's not really something I can discuss out here. Can I come in?'

'Um… I suppose.' He opened the door for her to come in, and led her through to the dining room, where the table had been cleared, ready for a séance.

'She has a session at four. She should be back any minute. What was it you wanted to see me about?'

Liz hesitated. It wasn't ideal that they were alone in the house – she should probably have abandoned her plan. But she was too curious to give up now.

'Do you mind if I have glass of water first? I'm quite thirsty.'

'Erm... okay.' He gave her a quizzical look, then started out the door towards the kitchen.

'Eddie!'

'What?' He turned.

Liz watched the emotions play over his face as he realised what had just happened. First confusion, then shock, then horror. Then something darker. He took a step towards her.

'Yoo hoo! I'm home.' Hilda called out from the hall. 'Come and give me a hand with these bags.'

Eddie stared at Liz, then went into the hall.

Liz slumped with relief. For a second there, she thought she was a goner. She heard muffled voices in the hall, then Hilda appeared in the doorway.

'Mrs McLuckie. What are you doing here?'

Eddie appeared behind her, shooting Liz a look of appeal.

'I came to get something from Graham,' she improvised. 'A recipe.'

Hilda looked at Eddie for confirmation.

'My cin... cinnamon shepherd's pie,' he stuttered.

'He mentioned it at the last séance, didn't you? Promised me the recipe.'

Eddie nodded.

'Oh. Okay, then.' Hilda took off her coat. 'I'll have to leave you both to it. I need to get changed. Can you unpack that shopping when you've done, Graham?'

When Hilda had gone, Liz looked at Eddie. She hadn't liked the expression on his face as he'd stepped towards her, but he looked quite different now. He looked desperate.

'Please don't tell her,' he said.

'Tell her what? That you're not who she thinks you are? Or that you killed your sister?'

He recoiled as if she'd slapped him. 'I didn't kill Clara.'

Liz frowned.

'Honestly, I didn't.' He sat at the table, and indicated she should sit, too. Liz hesitated, but sat. She didn't think he would do anything with Hilda in the house. Looking at him now, it was hard to believe he'd killed anyone. He had his head in his hands, a picture of misery.

'Do you want to start at the beginning?'

'Not particularly.'

'Won't it be a relief to tell someone, after all these years?'

He wiped his nose with his hand. He had changed a lot from the young man he'd once been. He'd lost all his hair, for a start, and grown a beard. It was something of a miracle Liz had recognised him from the locket photo, but his eyes had given him away. The eyes were the windows to the soul, and in Eddie's case, it was a troubled one.

'Why did you stage your own death?' she prompted.

'I owed money. A *lot* of money. To Phil Nethergate.'

Liz frowned. That was a name she knew, and didn't particularly like. She'd had a nasty run-in with Philip Nethergate in the autumn. Surely he wasn't old enough to have been wheeling and dealing in the 80s?

Graham saw her puzzled look. 'Not *young* Philip, *old* Phil. If you think the young one's a nasty piece of work, you should've seen his dad. He was a right bastard. I could have done a runner, but I knew he'd find me, wherever I went. So I made it look like I'd died.'

Liz's lip curled. She couldn't quite believe he'd put his family through that, just to save his own skin. His poor mother had died not knowing the truth.

'Where did you go?' she asked, in a tone she hoped didn't betray her disgust.

'Manchester. But eventually I ran into problems there too, so...'

'You came back.'

Eddie nodded. 'Old Phil Nethergate died in 2002. I reckoned it was safe to come back then, although, obviously, I couldn't just turn up as Eddie again. My very first night back I met Hilda, at the Esplanade. I know it sounds corny, but it was love at first sight.'

'But you didn't tell her the truth.'

'How could I? I was on the run from some nasty people in Manchester, and didn't want to put her in danger. After we'd been together a few months, she wanted to get married, but I couldn't. It wouldn't be legal to marry her under an assumed name. I couldn't do that to her.' He smiled wanly. 'She's still giving me grief about it.'

'What about Clara?'

'I knew she was still living here, obviously. I hated that she had no idea what had really happened – it tortured me – but there wasn't much I could do about it, was there? I just kept out of her way. Until—'

'The night she died.' Clara had phoned Iris and told her 'something terrible' had happened. She was betting that something terrible was Eddie.

He nodded. 'She came to the house. To see Hilda. Apparently, they'd had some kind of séance over at the Anchorage, and it had given her the idea she wanted to try to get in touch with Eddie – with me – to confirm her theory I'd been murdered.'

'By Roger Darnton.'

Eddie's eyes narrowed. She could see him trying to gauge how much she knew. He made a noncommittal noise, and continued.

'Anyway, Hilda wasn't in, thank God... but Clara recognised me. Straight away. After she got over her shock, she flew at me like a mad woman. Scratching and screaming. She was in floods of tears. I eventually managed to calm her down, and told her I was glad she knew, because now we could see more of each other. But she wasn't having that. She told me she'd never forgive me, then she left.'

They sat for a moment or two in silence. Poor Clara. Liz could completely understand why she couldn't forgive Eddie. There was a bump from somewhere above them – Hilda moving about upstairs. Liz knew she didn't have much time.

'So when did Roger Darnton recognise you?' she asked.

Eddie's eyes narrowed again. 'I don't know what you're talking about.'

Even though he'd lived much of his life in a lie, Eddie Bendelow was actually a terrible liar. Liz could see the truth behind his eyes. He knew exactly what she was talking about.

'Was Roger blackmailing you?'

Hilda bustled in. 'Graham, those bags are still in the hall.' She saw Liz. 'Oh. Are you still here?'

'I was just leaving.'

Eddie got to his feet. 'I'll do the bags.' He went into the hall. Liz was about to follow, when Hilda stopped her.

'You can join our little séance today if you like. We could try to get in touch with your husband again. There's still a possibility he hasn't crossed over into the light yet. It can sometimes take years, you know.'

Liz laughed. She couldn't help it. How could Hilda possibly know what was happening in the so-called afterlife? She had no idea what was going on in *this* one!

Hilda was puzzled by her outburst. 'Are you okay?'

Liz was about to make some excuse, when there was a loud clatter from somewhere in the house. She ran into the hall.

The bags were still where Hilda had left them, but the kitchen door was open. Liz ran into the kitchen.

'Where do you think you're going?' Hilda hurried after her.

The window over the sink was wide open, its curtains

fluttering in the breeze. She heard a crash outside, and then a muffled curse. After a second, a head popped up above the windowsill.

'It's okay, Mrs Mac.' Constable Williams was grinning from ear to ear. 'We've got him.'

23

'You shouldn't have gone in when you knew Hilda wasn't there. You almost gave us a heart attack.'

'Yes, well, it all turned out okay in the end, didn't it?'

'No thanks to you,' said Kevin.

Liz put her coffee cup down on the grubby interview room table. She'd drunk so much she had the jitters.

'What are you charging him with?' she asked.

'He's already confessed to killing Roger Darnton. We'll also charge him for the murder of Clara Bendelow.'

'I don't think he killed Clara.'

'What about the DNA under her fingernails?'

'Clara scratched him when they had a fight. When she realised who he was. It's all in my statement.'

'I haven't had the chance to read that yet. It's longer than *War and Peace*.' Kevin was thoughtful, then shook his head. 'I think you're barking up the wrong tree. What are the chances of there being *two* murderers? Both at the Anchorage?'

Liz knew he had a point. And yet... Eddie really was a terrible liar. She'd put money on the fact that he'd been telling her the truth when he said he hadn't killed Clara. She looked up at Kevin.

'You'll be letting Leah go now, I suppose?' she asked him. Every cloud had a silver lining.

'Yes. Her DNA sample will clear her anyway, when it comes through, but under the circumstances, I think we can let her go as soon as we've done the paperwork.'

'You'd better get on with it, then.'

'I suppose I'd better.' Kevin grinned. 'Would you like a lift home? I can ask Bill to drive you.'

'No, I'm okay, thanks. I need to stretch my legs.'

On her way out, she kept an eye open for Inspector Flint. In the four hours she'd spent at the station since Eddie's arrest, Flint had been conspicuous by her absence. Liz suspected she hadn't wanted to admit she was wrong, or apologise to her. Liz couldn't imagine Flint apologising for anything.

Liz walked home, enjoying the fresh salty air. Her mind was still churning. It wasn't just the coffee; it was a single question, repeating itself in her head – if Eddie hadn't suffocated Clara, who had? The key had to be in the timing. Clara had been killed just after the ill-fated séance that had led to Clara's discovery of Eddie. It had been pretty obvious that Clara had been pushing the planchette. Had someone else, as well as Roger Darnton, thought she was accusing them of murder? There hadn't even been a murder at that point.

Liz's eyes widened. There hadn't been a murder. But someone *had* died.

THE NEXT MORNING, Liz woke with a renewed sense of purpose. She'd already taken Nelson for his clifftop walk, and had started breakfast, before Niall came downstairs.

'How about fish for tea?' she asked him.

'That would be grand. Can you get enough for three? Leah's getting out this morning.'

He was still in his boxer shorts and T-shirt.

'Aren't you going to work?'

'I've called in sick again. I've decided to pack it in at the museum anyway.'

'Why?'

'I don't think I'm cut out for archaeology. Let's face it, I'm not even qualified.' That was true. Not only had he fudged his degree on his CV, but Liz had also had to blackmail Dora Spackle into giving him references. But he didn't know that. Maybe he was right. Maybe archaeology wasn't really his thing.

'So what are you going to do instead?' she asked.

He shrugged. 'For now, I can manage with the cash from the ghost tours and the Duke of York.' He hesitated. 'I thought might head back to Ireland in a few weeks.'

'Oh.' Liz couldn't hide her dismay.

'You've been very kind. But I have a better chance of getting a proper job back home.'

Liz nodded. 'Your mum must be missing you too. There's no place like home, is there?'

WHEN LIZ STEPPED out of Mike Howson's fish shop on Baxtergate an hour later, she'd obtained much more than the three haddock fillets she had in her shopping bag – she now had the growing conviction she was finally on the track of Clara's killer.

She turned the corner into Flowergate... straight into the path of Benedict Ossett.

'Oh!' she said.

'Liz!' He was equally wrong-footed, but she saw his surprise turn quickly into something else. Determination.

'I'm glad I bumped into you,' he said. 'Do you have a minute? We need to talk.'

'I'm sorry, B, but I really don't have the time right now.'

'I know you've been avoiding me.'

'I haven't,' she lied.

He arched an eyebrow.

She sighed. 'Okay. I admit it, I have been avoiding you, and yes, we do need to straighten things out. But not right now.'

'Straighten things out?' echoed Benedict. 'That's an odd way of putting it.'

'Sorry. I really am in a hurry. I have to go.' She side-stepped him and hurried on her way. She resisted the urge to look back over her shoulder, guessing he was still staring after her. She would deal with him, and their relationship... whatever it was... later. In the meantime, she really did have things to do, and she needed a clear head to do it.

JUST AFTER LIZ had returned to Gull Cottage, Niall got a phone call from Leah, and put his coat on to go and pick her up.

'I won't be here when you get back,' Liz said. 'I know you two have a lot to talk about.'

'We do.' Niall's brows knitted together. 'But I don't want to chase you out. It's your house.'

'I have stuff to do anyway.'

'Oh?' He looked more closely at her, and her determined expression. 'What kind of stuff?'

'I'll tell you later. Go and get your lady.' Then she had a thought. 'Can you give me a lift to the West Cliff on your way?'

. . .

LIZ RANG the doorbell at the house on East Terrace. She hoped Hilda was in, and that she would answer the door. Mike had told her in the fish shop (among other things) that Jessie in the Post Office had told him that Hilda had taken to her bed after Graham's arrest. Liz hoped she would be up and about again. She needed her.

The door was opened surprisingly quickly, by someone she didn't anticipate.

'Oh,' she said, taken aback. 'I wasn't expecting to see you here.'

Rose flashed her gold tooth. 'I bet you weren't, lovely. What can I do for you?'

'I need a word with Hilda.'

'No can do.' Rose's earrings jangled as she shook her head. 'She's fit for nothing. Is there anything I can help you with?'

Liz looked at her, speculative. It was possible there *was* something.

Rose read her expression. 'You'd better come in.' She led them into the hall, past the dining room door. 'Not in there,' she said. 'It has bad energy. Come into the living room.'

Liz followed her to the door at the end of the hall. The living room was dark, with bulky leather sofas and a feature wall built of grey stone. On one of the other walls there was a collection of knives. Najavas. Virtually identical to the ones in Rose's kiosk. There was one missing in the middle of the display – Liz could see the nail it had hung on.

'I don't understand,' said Liz.

Rose saw what had attracted her attention. 'Family heirlooms.'

Liz frowned.

'Hilly is my sister.'

'But...?'

'She married young. Good sort, but it didn't last long. All she was left with was the name.'

Something clicked into place in Liz's head. When she'd told Rose about the najava, Rose must have guessed where it had come from. But...

'Why did you throw a rock through the window?'

'Ah, you heard about that, did you? Not my finest hour.' Rose settled into an armchair, and indicated that Liz should do the same. 'Me and Hilly hadn't spoken for years. Not since she took up with that *gadje* of hers.'

'Graham?'

'Eddie.'

'You didn't *know* that, though, did you?'

'I knew there was something off about him. Seriously off. The cards told me. I tried to tell her, but she wouldn't listen. Words were said. Bad words. After that, we didn't speak for twenty years.'

Twenty years!

'We're proud folk,' said Rose, reading Liz's mind, or maybe just her face. 'We can hold a grudge for a lifetime. Longer. But when you told me about the najava, I knew her man had killed Roger Darnton. I tried to tell her, but she wouldn't even open the door. I knocked, and rang, and called through the letterbox. But she didn't answer. So I threw a rock through the window.' Rose laughed. 'That got her attention, right enough. And the *gavvers*.'

Liz guessed that was the police. Kevin, in fact.

'Why didn't you tell *him* about the knife?'

Rose shot Liz a look. 'Hilda is *familia*. I'd defend her with my life.'

But not speak to her for twenty years.

Liz's thoughts must have shown on her face, because Rose's expression hardened.

'What is it you're wanting her for anyway?'

'A favour.'

Rose's eyebrows shot up. She cackled. 'That's some brass neck you have. Wasn't it you set the *gavvers* on that man of hers?'

'Yes.' Liz pulled a rueful face. 'But I was hoping she might listen to me anyway. I really need her help.'

'Like I said, Hilly's out of action. On pills from the doctor. Good for nothing.'

'Maybe you can help me?'

'Maybe.'

'I need someone to run a séance.'

Rose frowned and shook her head. 'You're on your own there, lovely. That's not my cup of tea at all.'

'You don't believe in ghosts?'

'I do. They're real, right enough. But I don't believe in conjuring them for money.'

Liz looked at her slyly. 'I don't *have* to pay you.'

Rose laughed, long and hard. When she'd recovered, she wiped her eyes. 'Nice try, lovely. I don't believe in conjuring spirits for *any* reason, not for money, not for love. They come when they come. So if you don't mind, I'm going to say no to your very generous offer. No hard feelings, though?'

'No hard feelings.'

'In that case, I'll see you out.'

They went back into the hall. Rose was about to open the front door, when she stopped.

'I almost forgot, I have something for you. I got it last week.'

'For me?' Liz was surprised.

Rose disappeared into the kitchen. She was there for ages. Liz was wondering whether she shouldn't just let herself out, when she reappeared, and pressed an envelope into Liz's hand.

'There you go. A present.'

'Thank you.' Liz wondered what it could be. She went to rip it open. Rose stopped her.

'Not now, lovely. Save it for later. When you're on your own.'

'Okay.' Liz put it in her pocket.

Whatever it was, it could wait.

24

'If you don't mind me saying, you look quite young to be doing this sort of thing.'

'That's marvellously kind of you.' Renowned clairvoyant Professor Wilberforce Gough blinked at Violet Baxter through his thick spectacles. 'I can assure you I am older than I look.'

'Were you born with the sight?' asked Max Plum. 'Or is it something you've had to cultivate?'

'If you'd read my autobiography, *My Life in the Shadows,* you would know that I had my first clairvoyant experience when I was just five years old. Children are natural conduits, of course. In childhood, the veil between the living and the dead is very thin. But, sadly, it thickens as we age.'

'Excuse us just one minute.' Liz nodded to Violet and Max, and steered the professor to a corner of the dining room, where no one could hear them.

'*My Life in the Shadows*?' she hissed.

'Well they're not going to be able to google it, are they?' whispered Niall. 'Not before the séance, anyway.'

Irwin had done a tremendous job on Niall's disguise,

greying his hair in places, giving him a scrubby beard, and hiding his blue eyes between glasses so thick it made them look like blackcurrants. Niall waggled his newly bushy eyebrows.

'I thought it would add to my credibility.'

'Don't push your luck. Behave yourself.'

'Are you sure this is a good idea, Mrs McLuckie?' Patricia Haddington approached them. 'There have been a lot of deaths in here lately.' The usually doughty ex-solicitor looked slightly nervous.

'There have.' Dickie Ledgard was right behind her. 'Nasty ones, too. And I remember poor Mr Darnton saying séances could be dangerous.'

'THAT WAS OUIJA BOARDS HE WAS TALKING ABOUT.' Iris joined them, glass of gin in hand. 'NOT SÉANCES.'

'Well, of course,' said the professor, nodding sagely, 'a Ouija board is notoriously difficult to control. Spirits are like... cows.'

Cows? Liz flashed him a look.

'... or horses. You have to handle them carefully. You have to show them who's in charge. And protect yourself effectively, of course. Which is only possible through years of experience.'

The Third Eye Society, which had been without a venue or leadership since Eddie Bendelow's arrest, had jumped at the chance to hold their meeting at the Anchorage. They'd been even more delighted when they heard a guest clairvoyant had volunteered to lead it. Violet Baxter, on the other hand, had taken a little more persuasion. Liz had had to assure her the Society would make a financial contribution to the Anchorage summer outing. She hoped they would – she still had to speak to someone about that. If not, she'd have to put her hand in her own pocket. She just hoped it would be worth it

There were several people attending from the Third Eye Society that Liz didn't know, but some she did – the middle-aged couple who had wanted Roger Darnton to get in touch with their dead son, and the girl who had fainted. Together with Violet, a couple of the more adventurous residents of the Anchorage, plus Iris, Patricia, Max and Dickie, there were more than a dozen participants, all eager to see what spirits Professor Gough might conjure.

'Are we all ready?' demanded the professor. 'Shall we begin?'

Everyone made their way to the table. Actually, it was several tables, pushed together and covered with a collection of mismatched tablecloths. Liz went to the window. It was dark outside, even though it was only five o'clock – a typical Whitby winter evening. She made sure the curtains were tightly drawn, before heading to her own seat.

'Do we have to have it quite so gloomy in here?' asked Patricia. The room was lit only by a single standard lamp at the professor's shoulder. It cast odd shadows across the table and draped the corners of the room in darkness.

'Don't worry, my dear,' said the professor. 'We have to keep the level of illumination low to make the atmosphere conducive to etheric flow. But you are quite safe in my hands.'

'Come and sit here,' suggested Dickie, patting the chair beside him. 'Beside me and Mrs G.'

Patricia did as he suggested, so that Dickie's narrow frame was sandwiched between her and Iris. The professor looked around at the expectant faces.

'We should say a prayer before we begin,' he said. His black-currant eyes gleamed. 'Mrs McLuckie, will you do the honours?'

Very funny. Liz would make him pay for that later.

'Okay,' said Liz. 'Erm...'

Everyone closed their eyes.

'May the Lord bless everyone here tonight, and protect us. May he guide any poor lost souls towards the light of this table. And...' she hesitated, realising she was running out of ideas, '...amen.'

'Amen,' echoed everyone. They opened their eyes.

'Short but sweet,' said the professor. 'Thank you, Mrs McLuckie. Now, if we could all join hands in the circle?'

Everyone held hands. Liz was sitting between Max Plum and the fainting girl. Max had an iron grip, while the girl had a touch like a butterfly. Liz looked at her anxiously. She hoped she would stay conscious this time.

The professor frowned, took a deep breath in, held it, and let it out again in a long, resonant 'Ahhhhhh!' He did that several times.

In... and 'Ahhhhh!'

In... and 'Ahhhhh!'

His face smoothed.

'I think he's there,' whispered Violet. 'I think he's in the beyond.'

'Shhh,' hissed Max Plum. 'Don't break his concentration.'

Then the professor spoke, in a slow, stentorian tone. 'My spirit guide is with me now. How are you tonight, Mr Patel?' He cocked his head, as if listening to the answer. 'He says there are many spirits gathering to talk to us. Very well, Mr Patel, you may admit them to the circle.' He gave a sharp intake of breath that made the fainting girl flinch. Liz gripped her hand reassuringly.

'One at a time,' urged the professor to the imaginary hordes. 'One at a time, please. Yes, sir, what can I do for you?'

He cocked his head, listening.

'I have a gentleman here with a birthmark.' Niall waved

his hand vaguely over his face. 'A port wine birthmark over one eye.'

'What did he say?' hissed Dickie to Iris.

'HE SAID THERE'S A GENTLEMAN HERE WITH A BIRTHMARK.'

Liz winced. She hoped Iris wasn't going to spoil the atmosphere. But after a furtive glance around the table, she realised she needn't worry. Everyone was waiting, breathless, to hear what the professor would say next.

'The gentleman is called Michael...'

The middle-aged couple grasped each other's hands, hard.

Liz's heart sank. She should have warned Niall to steer clear of that name. Luckily, Niall spotted her look of horror.

'No.' He shook his head. 'Not Michael. Matthew. Matthew tells me he is looking for a little girl called Lizzie, who is here tonight.' He turned, as if addressing the spirit. 'I'm very sorry, sir, but you must be mistaken. There are no little girls here.'

'Actually,' piped up Liz, 'I think that might be me.' She didn't enjoy the deception, but she knew they had to make at least one convincing display of the professor's credentials before the main event. 'I had a great uncle Matthew, who had a birthmark on his forehead.'

A murmur of satisfaction ran round the table.

The professor's nodded. 'He says he's with your mother. She's very well and is asking after you.'

Liz's eyes prickled. Even though she knew it was nonsense – made up for their audience – she would have liked to have had a real message like that from her mum.

'Matthew is fading now... there's quite a bit of jostling here. Everyone wants to be heard. One at a time please. Oh... oh...'

Everyone leaned forward in their seats.

'There is someone else coming through. Very, very power-ful... I'm not sure I...'

Without warning, the light went out. There were several cries of consternation, that turned to relief a couple of seconds later, when it flickered back on again. Everyone exchanged excited looks.

'Argh!' The professor's face twisted, as if in the grip of some powerful emotion.

There was a collective intake of breath as a figure rose up behind his chair. She was mostly in darkness apart from her face, which was bone white. She had dark hair tucked under her starched white cap, and was dressed in an old-fashioned apron. A nurse's uniform.

Patricia gave an anguished cry. 'No!'

Everyone looked at her.

'No,' she gasped again. Her face was etched in lines of horror.

The ghostly nurse turned her eyes towards her.

Patricia put her hands over her face. 'Make her go away!'

But the professor was unresponsive, slumped over the table with his eyes closed. The whole table watched in horri-fied silence as the nurse slowly lifted her arm... and pointed her finger straight at Patricia.

'I'm sorry! I'm sorry!' gasped Patricia. 'I had to do it! I had to.' She jumped out of her chair, and backed away, until she was pressed against the wall and could go no further. 'I'm sorry!' she shrieked. 'I'm so sorry I killed you!'

She collapsed, sobbing, on the floor.

The overhead lights snapped on, making everyone blink. Kevin and DC Williams were standing just inside the door, by the light switch. The nurse's ghost grinned and patted Niall on the back.

'Good work, professor.'

Niall recovered and beamed back at her. 'Right back at you, nursie.'

'What in God's name is going on?' blustered Max. Everyone was gaping at Tilly and Niall, and at each other, in bewilderment.

Kevin marched over. 'Patricia Haddington, I am arresting you for the murder of Elizabeth Barker. You do not have to say anything. But, it may harm your defence if you do not mention when questioned something which you later rely on in court. Anything you do say may be given in evidence against you.'

'How DID you know it was her?' asked Violet Baxter. All the Third Eye guests had gone, Kevin had taken Patricia to the police station, and everyone else was recovering in the drawing room, in front of the fire.

'A process of elimination,' said Liz. 'I knew it had to be someone who was at that original session with the Ouija board. Someone who thought Clara knew they'd murdered Bessie. There was only three people it could have been – Patricia, Max or Dickie.'

'Me?' Dickie looked alarmed. He might be deaf in one ear, but he had no problem hearing *that*.

'DON'T WORRY.' Iris patted his hand. 'NO ONE THINKS YOU'RE A MURDERER.'

'That's a relief.'

Liz continued with her explanation. 'Patricia's mother died of a codeine overdose. Mike Howson told me, and Kevin confirmed it when he managed to unearth the original coroner's report. The coroner ruled it misadventure, even though her GP denied he'd prescribed enough codeine to kill her. Codeine wasn't easy to get hold of without prescription, but there was someone who did have easy access to it.'

'Bessie Barker!' thundered Max. 'A nurse!'

Liz nodded. 'Exactly. Patricia and Bessie were very close.' Liz wondered whether she should say she thought the two women might have been lovers, but decided not to. If they'd kept it secret for so many years, it wasn't her place to betray it. 'Patricia persuaded Bessie to help her kill Amanda Hadding-ton, just as Rose Young thought she had.'

'For money, I suppose.' Dickie shook his head sadly. 'It usually comes down to money, doesn't it?'

'Actually, no,' said Liz. 'Not in this case. Amanda's inheri-tance didn't go to Patricia, it went to a distant cousin. I think that's why she'd asked Patricia to come and see her. She knew she was dying and wanted to gloat that she wasn't going to give her a penny. It was too much for Patricia.'

'So it still did come down to money, really,' said Tilly, 'in the end.'

'I suppose.'

Everyone was silent, thinking about it.

'I DON'T UNDERSTAND,' said Iris. 'WHY DID SHE KILL BESSIE?'

'Because she had dementia,' said Liz. She looked at Violet for confirmation.

Violet nodded. 'Bessie was diagnosed a couple of years ago, but it had got much worse in the weeks before she died. She was telling everyone she had a secret.'

'Patricia thought she was going to betray her,' said Liz.

'How awful,' muttered Dickie. 'Poor Mrs Barker.'

'But,' said Tilly, 'isn't it possible she killed her out of love? It must be terrible to have to watch someone you love deteri-orate like that.'

Mags gave her a hug. She had been responsible for the momentary electricity outage that had given Tilly the chance to creep out of the store cupboard behind Niall, and crouch behind his chair. A prior visit to a theatrical costume suppliers in York and her remarkable resemblance to her distant relative – Bessie Barker – had done the rest.

'Whatever Patricia's motives,' said Liz, 'the result was the same. She killed Bessie, then she killed Clara, thinking Clara had somehow found out about it.'

'Maybe she thought Bessie had already told Clara her secret, about Amanda?' suggested Mags.

'Maybe,' said Liz. 'We might never find out.'

Tilly yawned and took off her cap to scratch her head. 'I don't know about the rest of you, but I'm knackered. It's been a hell of a night.'

Liz grinned. 'For some of us more than others.' She nodded to where Niall was asleep in an armchair, spectacles on his lap, mouth open, snoring.

'JUST LIKE MY IRWIN,' said Iris. 'HIS SNORES WOULD WAKE THE DEAD.' She grinned when she realised what she'd said, then cackled with laughter.

25

'To Leah!'

'LEAH!' Everyone raised their glasses.

'Happy travels!'

Leah blushed. 'Thanks, everyone. Cheers.'

They'd decorated the café with balloons and paper chains made by Lukasz and Eryk, who were now sitting at one of the tables, guzzling cake and drinking lemonade. Everyone else was drinking prosecco, except Iris, who hated THAT FIZZY MUCK, and was nursing a glass of gin.

'Where are you off to first?' asked Tilly, who was sitting with her arm around Mags.

'Bali, for a few months. From there, I'll push on to Australia.'

Iris shuddered. 'DON'T THEY HAVE RUDDY GREAT SPIDERS IN AUSTRALIA?'

Dickie patted her hand reassuringly. Lately, everywhere Iris went, Dickie went too. Everyone was delighted for them.

'Spiders?' Ten-year-old Lukasz stuck his up his head. 'We love spiders, don't we, Eryk? Can we come?'

'You are far too young to be going off to Australia,' said Gryzna. 'You have to go to school. Work hard.'

Lukasz blew a raspberry, which Gryzna wisely ignored. She knew she had to pick her battles, or she'd wear herself out.

'I don't suppose there's any more bubbly in that bottle?' asked Irwin, peering into his glass. 'Mine seems to have evaporated.'

Niall picked up the bottle. 'Nope. All gone.'

'Don't worry,' said Tilly, getting to her feet. 'There's plenty more where that came from.' She headed into the kitchen.

'I'll give you a hand, Tills.' Kevin followed her. He looked exhausted, having spent the last few weeks tying up loose ends and preparing the cases against Eddie Bendelow for the murder of Roger Darnton and Patricia Haddington for Clara's murder. Flint had – begrudgingly – spared him an hour to attend the party.

'We'll be seeing you again, Leah, I hope?' said Benedict, who had been unusually quiet. He rubbed Nelson's ears. For some reason, Nelson had stuck like glue to him ever since they'd arrived. Liz, on the other hand, had avoided even looking at him.

'Of course you will,' said Leah. 'You're not going to get rid of me that easily. I'll come back and see you all... and Niall, of course.' She winked at Niall.

Niall grinned back. They'd sorted out their differences, and he seemed to have taken her decision to continue her travels in his stride.

'Ta dah!' Tilly and Kevin reappeared through the beaded curtain with several more bottles of prosecco.

'Can you fill everyone's glasses again, please?' asked Niall. 'I have another toast.'

Kevin popped a cork, and topped up everyone.

Niall lifted his brimming glass. 'To Tilly and Mags, and their generosity.'

Tilly blushed. Everyone else looked at him. They all knew the two women were generous, but it sounded like he was talking about something specific.

'As you all know, I'm finished at the museum. And... I won't going back to Ireland.'

That was news to Liz.

'I'm off to college. Teeside College, to be exact, where I'll be studying Acting and the Performing Arts.'

'Oh, bravo!' Irwin clapped. 'Very well done!'

'That's great news!' said Liz.

'You were very good as Professor Gough,' said Tilly.

'And Doctor Darke,' chipped in Eryk. 'You were totally sick!'

Liz imagined that meant good. If so, he was right.

'I can only do it because of Tilly,' said Niall. 'She's lending me the money for my tuition fees.'

Tilly blushed again. 'Bessie's inheritance. What's left of it.'

Niall raised his glass again. 'To Tilly and Mags!'

'TILLY AND MAGS.'

Afterwards, as everyone was admiring Tilly and Mags's new coffee machine, Niall sidled up to Liz.

'Erm... I was wondering. Tilly's been really generous paying for my fees, but the student halls are pricey. Do you think—?'

'Of course!' Liz cut in. 'I'd be offended if you stayed anywhere else. You can commute to college from here, can't you?'

'I think Frannie can make it.'

Kevin approached them, bottle in hand. 'Do either of you need another top up?'

'I'm grand, thanks,' said Niall. He hurried off to put an arm around Leah's waist.

Liz grinned at Kevin. 'How're things at the station? Has Flint forgiven you yet?'

Kevin snorted. 'For now.' He looked at his watch and pulled a face. 'I'd better head back, though, or she'll go on the warpath again.'

The party continued after he left. Liz drank a little more than she should, and avoided Benedict assiduously. At times, she felt his eyes on her, but never acknowledged it. But when she stood up to get her coat, he was suddenly at her side.

'Can I walk you home?'

'No.' She realised that had come out rather more harshly than she intended. 'Sorry, B.' She glanced at the others, but they were all too intent on their own conversations to take any notice of theirs. She dropped her voice anyway, just to be sure. 'I just... I just don't know if I'm ready yet. You understand, don't you?'

He nodded. 'Yes. Of course.' But he was lying. Benedict had a tell, one that she'd come to recognise during their many evenings playing Mah-jong. Whenever he bluffed, or told a lie, the left-hand corner of his mouth would twitch. It was a dead giveaway, and one he was entirely unable to control. His mouth had just twitched. Liz wanted to kiss it, but resisted the temptation.

Really, it was better if they didn't go there again.

She said her good nights to everyone else and stepped out into the chilly air. It was only a few minutes' walk home to Henrietta Street, and she was determined not to spend them mooning over Benedict. She thought about Niall instead. She was delighted for him. He really had a talent for acting, which would be totally wasted in a dusty museum. She was delighted for herself, too, that she'd still have him living with her at Gull Cottage. She'd grown so used to having him around. It would be lonely on her own.

Yip yip!

Nelson greeted her as she let herself in. She smiled. No, not lonely. Never lonely, when she had the ugliest dog in Yorkshire to keep her company! Liz hugged him. He was the cleverest dog in Yorkshire too. She would never have found Clara's locket, and the photo of Eddie, without his help.

'Good boy! How about a doggy treat?'

He wagged his tail.

'Okay, sweetie, let me get my coat off first.'

As she was taking her coat off, she felt something crackle in one of the pockets. The envelope Rose had given her weeks earlier, just before their séance at the Anchorage. With all the drama that had happened since, she had completely forgotten about it. She took it out and opened it.

There was a Tarot card inside. It showed an illustration of a spoked wheel, with a number of odd-looking animals strapped to it. Underneath it said *Wheel of Fortune*. It was accompanied by a hand-written note.

The wheel falls... then rises again. The cycle repeats, as surely as spring follows winter. Only an idiot would choose to live in winter forever. Oh, and by the way, you'll find what you've been looking for behind the dresser in your bedroom.

Happy Valentine,
Rose x

Liz frowned. She'd had quite enough of mumbo-jumbo, thank you very much! And hadn't Rose given her the envelope *after* Valentine's Day?

But she was curious.

She pushed the envelope back into her pocket, and went upstairs to her bedroom. Her dresser was an old Scottish chest of drawers where she kept her jewellery box and make-up. It was Victorian, and still had its original chipped and shabby paint, but Liz liked it because she'd inherited it from her gran.

It took a fair bit of effort for her to pull it away from the wall. She peered behind. At first she couldn't see anything, but as her eyes adjusted she spotted something lying on the floor, beside the skirting board. She just managed to slide her arm down between the chest and the wall to pull it out. It lay in the palm of her hand, tangled with fluff but otherwise undamaged. Her missing ruby earring. The earring Mark had bought her for Valentine's Day.

Happy Valentine.

She stared at it. How on earth had Rose known it was there? Liz sat on the bed, and took the Tarot card and note back out of her pocket. The illustration on the card looked medieval – the animals strapped to the wheel weren't recognisable as anything in particular, and wore silly, almost human, expressions.

The cycle repeats, as surely as spring follows winter. Only an idiot would choose to live in winter forever.

Liz thought about her friends. About Niall, about to embark on an exciting new career, and Leah, who'd put her terrible experiences in Whitby behind her and was heading off on another adventure. She thought about Gryzya, who had courageously fled Belarus to start a new life in the UK, and Iris, who, in spite of her age, was taking a chance on the Anchorage, and – by the look of it – on Dickie, too.

Finally, she thought about Benedict. There was no doubt he had loved his wife Katherine, but his grief hadn't frozen him solid. He was still open to possibilities, and was prepared to take another chance.

On her.

Was she the only one who couldn't move forward? Was

she frozen by grief, or by fear? She'd never thought of herself as a timid person.

She went back downstairs. Nelson had given up on the treat she'd promised him, and was curled up in his basket, with an assortment of Clara's clothes he'd selected from the pile in the corner. He looked so comfortable she didn't have the heart to take them off him.

She sat for a minute. Thinking. Then she took out her mobile phone and dialled. It was answered on the third ring.

'Liz?'

'Hi, B. Are you still at the party?'

'No. I decided to call it a night. I'm back home.'

She took a deep breath. 'Is it okay if come over?'

AUTHOR'S NOTE

Whitby is, of course, a real place – a gorgeous jewel of a town nestled on the North Yorkshire coast, on the edge of the North York Moors National Park. It's most famous for being the birthplace of colonial explorer Captain Cook, and the inspiration for Bram Stoker's gothic masterpiece *Dracula*. For those of you lucky enough to be familiar with the town, I've done my best to keep its geography – its street names and layout – as close to the real thing as possible. I may, however, have made a few mistakes and taken a couple of liberties, for which I hope you'll forgive me.

I haven't used as many real places in this book as I have in my previous ones, although Kipper Cottage and Gull Cottage are based on the two cottages closest to Fortune's Smokehouse, on Henrietta Street. Neptune Yard is my own version of Kiln Yard, which can be found through an iron gate at the foot of the 199 steps. The Full Moon Café and the Anchorage Retirement Home are my own inventions.

The Third Eye Society is also fictional. I don't know if there's a real-life spiritualist group based in Whitby, and if there is, I hope they won't be offended. Hilda Blakey, Roger

Darnton and Professor Willoughby Gough might all be fakes, but that doesn't mean all mediums are. I actually believe in ghosts. Sort of.

All my characters are, of course, fictional, except for Kipper Cottage guests Helen and Andrew and their French bulldog Hugo, who have made a guest appearance.

Finally, I'd like to thank born-and-bred Whitby 'east ender' Lesley, for providing the saying 'first one up gets the shoes', and for her entertaining, real-life stories about Whitby and her Uncle Dave, better known in Whitby's fishing community as 'Crock'.

I hope you've enjoyed spending time in Whitby with Liz McLuckie, and that you'll join her for her next adventure in the Kipper Cottage Mystery series – *Death on the Stella Mae*.

Until then, happy armchair sleuthing!

If you'd care to leave a review on Amazon they are enormously helpful in getting books discovered by new readers and I would be grateful for you thoughts.

ABOUT THE AUTHOR

Jan lives just outside Edinburgh with her husband, three kids, a one-eye whippet and a fat black pug. Born in a colliery village in the North East of England, she cut her literary teeth on the great storytellers of the 60's and 70's - Wilbur Smith, Frank Yerby, Mary Renault, and Sergeanne Golon. She began her writing career as an advertising copywriter, and has since had novels published by Random House and HarperCollins, and original audio series produced by Audible UK. She also writes for tv.

Jan enjoys psychological thrillers and crime fiction of all kinds, from the coziest of cozies to the blackest of noirs.

You can find Jan at www.kippercottagemysteries.co.uk

ALSO BY JAN DURHAM

Kipper Cottage Mysteries

Death at the Abbey (Book 1)

Death at Neptune Yard (Book 2)

Death at the Feast (Book 3)

Death at the Anchorage (Book 4)

Death on the Stella Mae (Book 5)

Printed in Great Britain
by Amazon

23031935R00128